Sasi is waiting

AND OTHER STORIES BY **SUJATHA**

Sasi is waiting

AND OTHER STORIES BY **SUJATHA**

Translator
Vimala Balakrishnan

GLOBAL
COLLECTIVE
PUBLISHERS

Published by Global Collective Publishers
16 North Bryn Mawr Avenue, #1355
Bryn Mawr, PA 19010 U.S.A.
www.globalcollectivepublishers.com

First published in India by Vitasta Publishing Pvt Ltd

Paperback ISBN: 978-1-954021-65-5
eBook ISBN: 978-1-954021-66-2

Cover painting: K R Santhanakrishnan
Cover and layout: Somesh Kumar Mishra

CONTENTS

PUBLISHER'S NOTE

In our quest to bring vernacular literature to the mainstream through our Relive Series (*Reliving Indira Goswami and Reliving Tagore*), we came across S Rangarajan who penned under his wife's name Sujatha. He has been one of the most popular writers of Tamil fiction and has also been featured in several magazines.

Later he contributed as script/screenplay writer for several Tamil movies. He also immortalized Ganesh-Vasanth—an imaginary advocate pair serving as the main characters in most of his detective stories. In the movie *Priya*, his fictional character Ganesh was played by Rajnikanth. Kamal Haasan's *Vikram* was composed by him. He penned dialogues for the movie *Roja* directed by Mani Ratnam.

It is our firm belief that India's regional literature is at par with literature from any other part of the world. We are fortunate that our belief only grows stronger with every passing day when we see the response to *Reliving Sujatha Volume I.* It is our great pleasure to announce that we have come up with another volume titled '*Sasi is Waiting and Other Stories by Sujatha*'. The stories are translated by Vimala Balakrishnan and edited by Veena Batra. These stories catch the reader unawares with unexpected twists and turns filling them with awe, shock and horror. Through this book, we hope that readers will relive the legacy of Sujatha's special art of storytelling.

SASI IS WAITING
AND OTHER STORIES

The Traveller

The security check at the airport was quite rigorous due to the recent hijack threats of various planes. The gentleman who went inside the security cabin was thoroughly screened by opening his suitcase and emptying it. The inspector did not spare even the soap case and hair oil, frisked him thoroughly and then stamped his boarding card with a victorious smile.

The passenger said with unconcealed irritation and anger, "Hope you didn't find any pistol in my bag. Are you satisfied now?"

The inspector said gracefully and with a pleasant smile, "With due apologies, I am only discharging my duty."

The passenger retorted, "Yes, you will harass the genuine travellers and will fail to nab the potential hijackers. Police force without imagination!"

The inspector gestured to me to come forward for security check unruffled by the recent outburst of the previous passenger.

This story is about the passenger who was before me and who had to undergo the rigorous scrutiny at the security booth. Excuse me for a minute till my security is cleared.

I met the gentleman again. He was smoking and had the *Time* magazine in his hand. He looked at his watch every few minutes.The irritation which he felt due to the recent harassment from the security personnel still lingered in his memory and his face mirrored the disgust that he felt. I was sitting next to him and he looked at me with the same disgust.

He was around fifty years old, and was fairly tall with a matching healthy physique. His eyes were clear and sharp and he had a straight nose. He might have been quite handsome when he was young. Had he dyed his hair and done something for the dark circles under his eyes, he would look very graceful. Though he was a chain smoker, his lips were not adversely affected. A majestic personality indeed! The Boeing seat was small for him. The way he sat commanded respect. It gave the impression that whatever happened around should have him as the focal point. A negligible delay of even a fraction of a second irritated him. He had no patience with those who stood in his way and his busy schedule. He did not tolerate any compromise where his comforts were concerned. His posture was a testimony to all these above mentioned characteristics.

The moment boarding was announced, he jumped up from his seat, walked up to the entrance like a young lad and inhaled the cigarette to the last puff before throwing it away. Then he hurried to the aircraft. His action indicated that everybody should emulate him. He disappeared from my sight temporarily.

I identified my green bag near the aircraft, climbed the steps leisurely, acknowledged the welcoming smile of the airhostess and sat on my allotted seat. When I looked around, I saw him sitting in my left side row. His expression seemed to say, why is everybody taking such a long time to board the aircraft.

Finally the flight took off at twenty to seven instead of ten past six. The flight attendant apologised for the delay and began the routine announcement, "Good evening, Ladies and Gentlemen. Welcome aboard IC flight 504...."

I fastened my seat belt and picked up the newspaper with the crossword puzzle. That's the best way to pass time during air travel.

The plane taxied down the runway gaining speed and climbed up at a steep incline. It turned, leaving behind Bangalore city which looked like a toy city through the window, chased the clouds and climbed up steadily covering thousands and thousands of feet.

The moment 'No smoking' was switched off, he lighted a cigarette. He was sitting in a non-smoking row. Immediately, his khadi-clad neighbour raised an objection. I could not make out their argument due to the aircraft's jet noise. I watched the scene with great interest as if it was a silent movie.

He was adamant and would not stub out his cigarette. His khadi-clad neighbour was equally adamant not to allow smoking. Indeed, a big problem! The button above the head was buzzed and the airhostess was summoned. She tried to mediate between the two in a soft and gentle but persuasive manner, but to no avail. Then she came and requested the lady sitting next to me to change her seat with the cigarette-smoking gentleman.

Hence, he came with his briefcase and sat next to me without extinguishing his cigarette. He looked at me with little grace and said, "Young man, do you have any objection if I smoke?" I smiled and said, "I can't object because this is not a non-smoking row." After this brief outburst, he completely ignored me only to blurt out, "What sort of people!" It was a general statement. I thought that had it been possible, he would have pulverised the man in khadi into a cigarette and smoked him with great satisfaction and relish. His ferocity could be discerned by the protruding veins on his forehead.

I wanted to go to the washroom but I was scared to make a move as I was sitting in the window seat and he was occupying the aisle seat.

The flight landed at Hyderabad after forty-five minutes. He took out a tablet from his briefcase and swallowed it with a glass of water given by the airhostess. Normally, I used to get off the aircraft and stretch my legs for a few minutes. I could not leave without making him get up. I was scared that he may burn me to ashes by his mere looks if I as much as mentioned that to him. Many people climbed down and stretched their legs. But I didn't have that much courage.

The flight did not take off in time from Hyderabad. It was badly delayed. Even after all the new passengers were seated, the door was not closed. A security personnel in white was walking up and down. Due to an oversight, there was an extra passenger. They were trying to find a seat for him.

He conceded to talk to me in frustration. "Why are they taking this much of time to take off?"

"The flight is full. There is no seat for a passenger."

"How stupid! They can't even run a normal flight efficiently!"

He called the airhostess. She came with a pleasant smile. "Why the delay?"

"Sorry. We will leave just now."

"If there is no seat for the passenger, ask him to leave and take off at once. Why do you torture the other passengers?"

"Sorry for the inconvenience. We will leave just now."

"At this rate, we will be in Delhi only by 11. I have to be in Delhi by 9.30. I have to catch another flight by Air India. I am in a bloody hurry Miss!"

"Forgive us. We will take off very soon." She changed the same refrain slightly. She left the place quickly so as to avoid any more harassment.

They managed to remove the extra passenger from the flight with great difficulty. Thank God! I thought, the plane would take off immediately. No! The door still remained opened. A white-uniformed man took the mike from the airhostess and announced with a strong Telugu accent, "Your attention please: Five boxes are not identified by the passengers. Passengers who have not identified their baggage are requested to come immediately and identify their baggage. Otherwise, they would be de-boarded."

The passenger lost his patience completely. He called the airhostess and screamed at her, "How can you run an airline this badly? It is already half past eight. I have to catch an Air India flight at 10.30. They won't wait for me. Why do you trouble people like this?"

"Sorry Sir, just a couple of minutes more."

"Call the captain! Call him at once!"

"If I call him, it will get further delayed." The airhostess replied with patience.

I applauded her composed manner against this sort of tirade. Her charming smile didn't leave her face even for a second. It was definitely a miracle!

Out of the five boxes, four were identified. The one which was not identified was brought into the aircraft and shown to each and every passenger for identification. The owner of the box was happily hiding behind a film magazine and having a gala time with his newly-wedded wife. He looked extremely sheepish and said, "Sorry, I didn't pay attention to the announcement."

The passenger, who was already in a lousy mood said, "These people should be sent to prison under MISA."

At last, the flight took off from Hyderabad. He looked at his watch and asked me, "What is the correct time?"

I said, "It is twenty past eight."

He said, "I am definitely going to miss the flight."

"When does it leave?"

"Half past ten."

"This flight would reach Delhi by 10.05. You have twenty-five minutes."

"But there is customs and security clearance."

"Don't worry. That flight also may get delayed like our flight."

"Air India is not this bad."

"Where are you going?"

"Moscow. There is a conference tomorrow. I have to be there positively."

"Don't be flustered."

"The whole system is very bad. I have travelled by many airlines in Europe. It was never this bad."

"What to do? The fear of being hijacked and the safety of passengers have led to this strict security vigil."

"Shit!"

As soon as the aircraft reached the desired stable level, snacks were served in plastic plates. He asked the airhostess to find out from the captain the exact time the flight would land in Delhi. He also told her to radio a message to Air India about a passenger to Moscow on this flight. She went in with some doubts.

"Useless girl! Do you know how smart the Lufthansa girls are? See what they have given for snacks. Don't know what oil they might have used! Salad…? For the money we pay…!"

It happened at that moment. It happened very silently. He stopped eating all of a sudden.

He pulled down his tie savagely and leaned on the seat.

I didn't notice it at first. I was eating. I noticed the strange unnatural sound from him only after an undue lapse of time.

His whole body was soaked in sweat. He gestured me to come closer to him. He looked very pale due to the excruciating pain. The pain was clearly visible and could be gauged by his crinkled eyebrows and the contracted facial muscles. He wanted to tell me something. He was pressing his chest with all his strength. With great difficulty and unseeing eyes he said, "Tablet" in a very feeble voice. His lips trembled as he said the word tablet.

I was not prepared for such an emergency. He was sitting in an unusual manner. I called the airhostess. I loosened his shirt and picked up the briefcase next to his legs. His body was cold. It happened suddenly and very silently without any pre-warning. Nobody was aware of what was happening. Even the passengers who were close by were having their meals unaware of the tragedy taking place. I had never seen a face with that much of pain and sweat in my life.

I opened the medicine bottle with shivering

hands as I had to give the tablet to the passenger along with the water brought by the airhostess. I opened his mouth…no, could not open it…. The water trickled down from his mouth. How cold! The body….

The hostess asked the passengers to vacate the front seats, folded the hand rests and made him lie down. She ran and made an announcement on the mike, "Attention please! If there is a doctor on board, please come immediately to the front portion….To the front portion."

Ripples! I pressed the air vent and made the cold air blow on his face.

"Open the buttons."

"Don't switch on the fan."

"Straighten the legs."

"Does anyone know how to give artificial respiration?"

"Don't let him lie down."

"Keep a pillow under his head."

"Cardiac arrest! Killer!"

"What? No doctor? Among so many passengers is there not a single doctor?"

Again the announcement over the mike! "Doctor, doctor please!"

His face was calm and composed. The

mouth was slightly parted. I felt his heart. It was cold. I searched for the heartbeat.

I saw the tear-filled eyes of the airhostess.

When I alighted slowly like a fallen leaf, I saw a white ambulance going towards the aircraft.

The loudspeaker was blaring in different places. "This is the last call for Dr Arvindan, passenger to Moscow by Air India flight…."

Yes, that was him! Dr Arvindan MD; MRCP (London); MRCP (Edinburgh)…. How many medical degrees!

Satellite

Pattabhiraman left for his evening stroll as usual, a habit which he picked up post his retirement about ten years earlier. Since then, he rarely missed this ritual. Pattabhiraman wanted to live for a long time. The doctor said that walking three miles per day increased longevity. He had read the same in *Reader's Digest* also. He used to go outside the city, cross the open field and reach the undulating high ground. This was his favourite place for the evening walk.

There would be no one else at the time he went for a walk. He was always alone. He found it easier to talk to himself aloud at this time. Occasionally, he used to get the nagging doubt that his wife, daughter and son were waiting for his death. He found it easier to argue in favour as well as against it when he was alone. Besides, he liked to walk on the soft grass. He could reminiscence about his past and walk in peace without the fear of traffic. He followed this practice almost every day.

It was just an ordinary evening. As usual, it was eighteen minutes past five. He had a muffler around his neck, a walking stick and canvas shoes. As was customary, he was talking to himself.

Unlike any other day, he had a strange experience that day. The recent rains had helped the grass to overgrow and hence, the whole place was a nice bright green. As he was walking on the lush green, he heard a 'whoosh' noise coming from above and behind him. He didn't pay any attention to the noise at first. But the unusual and unique 'whoosh' sound definitely drew his attention. There was no word in the language to describe it. The noise sent a chill down the spine of his body. He turned around. He could not see anything. He looked up and shuddered.

Around three hundred feet above the ground, he saw a self-rotating sphere which was slowly landing not straight but slightly at an angle. A very fine specimen of a sphere! It was made of a very bright and shining material. The metal had a tinge of blue. An amber light blinked by the side. Probably, a window!

Pattabhiraman was bewildered and stared at the sphere with his mouth wide open. He didn't realise he had dropped his walking stick.

The sphere slowly slid in front of him and landed about three hundred feet away from him. As it came down, it exhaled deeply. It made a noise, 'vroom, vroom, vroom'.... Two feet-like appliances ejected from the sides; its whirring noise increased. The feet-like appliances got planted firmly on the ground. The sphere stood firmly and steadily after a severe jerk-like motion. Now the 'whirring' sound was steady.

Its circumference was almost forty feet. It came to a halt and the 'whirring' noise stopped. Pattabhiraman had never seen such an object either in his real life or in any film. He wiped his glasses to get a better view. The first thought that occurred to him was that it was an experimental aircraft of the air force. But he had never seen any aeroplane with a spherical shape. He was a retired judge. Even with his basic scientific knowledge he knew that nobody could fly such a shape.

He looked around him to find out whether anybody else was there. Finding nobody, he felt a bit scared. But his curiosity to know what the object was made him stand rooted to the place.

Just then a small gate-like aperture opened and an object similar to a ladder was projected and placed on the ground. To Pattabhiraman it looked like a tongue sticking out. He could feel his heart beating very fast. From the sphere, an object came down the ladder. You have to call that object only a 'thing'. It definitely did not have the shape of a human being. The nearest comparison could be an eight-foot long fountain pen displayed for advertisement. An object resembling a fountain pen came down jumping, trembled for a few moments as in a cartoon show and then stood firmly. A little later, another similar object came down jumping.

It stood next to the creature that had landed first. Pattabhiraman wanted to run away from that place after picking up his dropped walking stick. At that moment he heard in English... "O man of the world, we are friends." The voice came from the sphere. The voice sounded like a computer's but afflicted with a cold. It was not natural like a human being's but was artificial.

The voice spoke without any modulations. Though Pattabhiraman was flabbergasted, his first instinct was to run away from the scene. He felt he would be more confident if only somebody was with him.

Is it possible to run when you are sixty-three? But I can walk away very quickly. He started walking as if in a hurry.

The 'fountain pen' said, "Don't be scared. We won't harm you. We have come as friends. Come! Come inside! Please come inside! Please do come inside positively! You will come, won't you?"

Pattabhiraman hesitated for a moment. He could see brightly-lit lights inside the open door. Both the 'fountain pen' friends were standing still. They did not seem to be frequent visitors to this planet. He decided to move closer to have a better look and took three steps.

"Excellent! Friend, come closer."

Pattabhiraman moved slowly towards it.

After thirty minutes, Pattabhiraman was walking quickly on the main road. He tried to stop all the vehicles going into the town to get a lift. A lorry stopped and the driver agreed to drop him at the bus stand. He got into the lorry. The lorry driver was slightly drunk. Pattabhiraman was not aware of it. He said, "Do you know what I saw just now?"

The lorry driver said, "Sir?"

"Me…just now…I saw aliens descending on earth. They have landed in the open field. They are all from a different planet."

"Is it so? How much does sugar cost there?"

"They are not human beings but men of a strange shape and size!"

"Who is a human being now? Tell me, are you a man? Am I a man? Who is a man? Everybody is corrupt."

Pattabhiraman did not try to convince or make the lorry driver understand anymore. He didn't have much time at his disposal. They had mentioned that they would wait exactly for an hour. Pattabhiraman wanted to share this wonderful and strange news with some more people. He wanted them to see this unique object. Who all to call? He could call his daughter. He could inform some VIPs of the city who were willing to come at such short notice. He had to invite the press people. He wondered whether to call reporter Sama Rao who would be at the City Club playing cards and also inform the police. Was it prudent to give them a hint about what they were about to witness? Pattabhiraman realised that it may take a while for them to reach the site and also get five to six people as witnesses. He decided to use his car.

Gopalan Nair wondered why Pattabhiraman was rushing home in a great hurry. As soon as he reached home, he called his daughter, "Revati, Revati." Revati who was reading the *Femina* walked in leisurely.

"What is it Dad?"

"Let's go immediately. Get the camera and the flash which are in the upstairs room."

"What's the matter?"

"Revati, something very exciting! I am going to show you something in the open ground outside the city. Bring the car out immediately."

Pattabhiraman's wife who came in just then said, "Why do you need the car? MD Ramanathan's concert is scheduled at the Town Hall in the evening. Why do you gasp like this? Did you run?"

Pattabhiraman ran towards the telephone. He dialled the City Club's number in a hurry. Both his wife and daughter stared at him puzzled.

"What is it, Dad?"

“What is it, dear?”

“Aliens from a satellite have landed. They are from outer space.”

They looked at each other.

“Hello, City Club? Pattabhiraman here! Sama Rao would be playing cards in the Bridge Room. Please call him. It is very urgent.”

“What are you blabbering? Are you not well?”

“Revati, quick bring the camera.”

“Why dad?”

“Hello! Hello Sama Rao! Pattabhiraman here! I’ve a big scoop for you.”

“Sama Rao! Listen carefully. The greatest scoop in the history of journalism! Space! Don’t you know space? Outerspace? Some people have come from outer space and landed near our city. In a spaceship! They are still there. They will be there for an hour. They speak English. They have a translating machine and spoke with me. There are eight people. They don’t resemble us. Some sort of long objects just like a pole. What? Me? No, I’m not drunk. Sama Rao, don’t be silly! I’m talking seriously. Bridge? Damn your bridge! Sama Rao, have I ever joked with you? I asked them to wait. They have agreed to wait. Just come with me.

I'll come and pick you up. I'll bring a camera. I'm calling you mainly because you belong to the press fraternity. I'll be there in ten minutes. Be ready."

He took a deep breath after putting the telephone receiver down.

"What happened to him today?"

"Wait mom. What did you see Dad?"

"Where is the camera? Bring it quickly."

"What's this Dad?"

"I have been shouting this long, don't you understand? Some aliens from outer space have landed in the open field just outside the city limit. I saw them with my own eyes. I went inside."

"Inside? What are you talking about?"

"They have landed in a spherical-shaped spaceship. I went inside that spaceship. What a surprise! Where is Ravi? Let him join us."

"What is this? He has never spoken like this. Dear…did you take your medicines today?"

"Chi! Why do you waste time like this? Don't you believe what I say? You people don't believe what I saw."

"Dad, what you say is confusing us very much."

"All your confusions will be resolved soon.

You bring out the car. I know it is very difficult to believe what I say. But, if you see that once, you will believe my words and everything will become clear. That is why I came running quickly. Nobody would believe me if I'm the only one who saw 'that'. I wanted another five or six people to see that object, so that the news will have some credibility. Quick, take out the car."

"Lord Venkateswara, what has happened to him?"

"Hey, stop lamenting, Revati you…." The look which he gave her proved he was very angry. Revati went towards the shed with perplexity written large on her face.

Sama Rao did not come out of the City Club in spite of the repeated honking. Pattabhiraman went inside in disgust and pulled Sama Rao away from the card game.

"Pattabhi Sir, are you serious?"

"Don't be silly! Come man… I'll show you."

"Tell me if it's a joke. I could not make out half of what you said over the telephone. Something about outer space, this and that…."

"Sama Rao, do you have eyes? Would you believe me if you saw that? Come I say. I'll show you! If you are the first one to report this, overnight you will be a rich man. 'Dame Luck', she is waiting for you. Hurry up!"

He pushed an open-mouthed Sama Rao into the car. Is Rajaratnam there?"

"Yes, he is inside."

"Call him! Wait. I'll drag him out. At least five of us can witness this."

Sama who was in the car said, "Aunty, what is this? Why is uncle talking like this? Besides, he has brought the camera also."

"It has happened all of a sudden. He has gone mad. If you question him, he roars in fury, like a lion."

"Mom, stop it. Mom, Dad has seen something strange otherwise he would not act like this. Let's see what it is."

"Pattu said that a person is afflicted with slight mental imbalance at the age of sixty-five or sixty-six. Her husband woke up in the middle of the night and made a *rangoli*. Has anybody cast an evil spell on him?"

"Mom, keep quiet! Dad is not afflicted by any such things."

Pattabhiraman dragged a surprised Rajaratnam with shoes in his hand, stuffed him inside the car and said, "Revati, quick! Start the car."

When they reached the place, the sun had set. The ground was crystal clear. As far as the eye could see, the ground was empty. 'It' could not be found. Pattabhiraman said, "Here, here only! I remember very well. I turned on the third milestone. Here! Positively here only!"

"Here! What?"

"It had landed here, in this place."

"What?"

"That ship."

"Pattabhi Sir!"

"Lord Venkateswara!"

"Dad what has happened to you?"

"Pattabhi, you have not yet told me why you dragged me out?"

"Pattabhi Sir, ship? A spaceship?"

"Somebody has cast an evil spell on him! Black magic!"

"Sama Rao, I saw it here. It landed here from the sky making a *whoosh* noise. Two projections like legs came out. The door opened. Two people got down. They called me. I went inside. How many different lights inside! Red, yellow and green! They talked like a machine but in a friendly way. They said they would be here for an hour. They wanted me to bring some more people. What's the time? It's only twenty past six. Have they left already? They said that they would wait. Let me see whether I can find any landing prints. Sama Rao, let's look for the landing marks …Sama Rao, Rajaratnam, Revati…." The four of them were just looking at him.

For the next few days, Pattabhiraman suffered a lot. Whenever he described what he saw that evening, people stared at him in a strange way. Pattabhi's wife very frequently told him, "Lie down and take rest," and secretly invoked Lord Venkateswara. Pattabhiraman wrote a letter to *The Hindu* describing in detail what he saw that evening. The letter was not published.

People started mumbling behind his back when he walked in the street. "All of a sudden something has happened. Till last week, he was all right….Probably he is possessed by a devil."

A doctor was called in by Ravi and Revati. The doctor said that he wanted to have a chat with him. Pattabhi heard the doctor saying as he was leaving, "This is a serious case. Shock treatment is advised. Take him to Madras. I'll give a reference letter to Dr Chakrapani."

Nobody believed him. Pattabhi felt sad and felt the fear surface once again. He feared that everybody would pack him off to a mental hospital if he continued talking about this. He wrote in his diary a 100 times, 'I saw it, I saw it' and hid it away safely where it was not easily found.

He wrote a letter to the central government's department of space. No reply. He always thought about it and occasionally stared with non-seeing eyes, either while eating or reading a newspaper. He stopped his evening walks completely.

On a particular evening, some new events took place in his house. A priest came. He had a chain which was made of big betel-nut sized beads. He removed the carpet in the hall and arranged small twigs, lighted them and placed a picture of Lord Hanuman by the side. He started chanting hymns after placing the other ingredients like milk, flowers, pomegranates, lighted incense sticks and fragrant benzoin gum (*sambrani*). Pattabhiraman, who came down from his room which was upstairs asked his wife, "What is all this?"

"Puja."

"What puja? Why puja?

"Hanuman puja, so that evil spirit won't enter into the house."

"If you wear a talisman, all your *brahmahathi* (grave sins) will get negated."

The priest continued his chants keeping a suspicious glance on him.

"*Brahmahathi* for whom? There is nothing wrong with me. *Brahmahathi* for you all. For you Revati, Ravi, Sama Rao and for this tuft-haired priest!"

The priest said, "Aunty, be careful. He may thrash you with whatever comes in his hand. Move away from there."

Pattabhiraman chased the pandit all over the hall resulting in his running away outside with the tucked fold of the *dhoti* coming loose leading to a big crowd in front of his house.

When Pattabhi went upstairs, his body shivered. I cannot destroy myself. All these people drive me crazy. Why? Is it because I keep speaking about that incident? Pattabhi forget it. Be normal and easy going. Never speak or think about that incident.

Pattabhi wore the muffler around his neck, put on the canvas shoes and took his walking stick. Both his wife and daughter were standing frightened on the landing. He resumed his evening walk which was stopped abruptly earlier saying, "I'm going for my walk" as if nothing had happened.

He walked normally without bothering about anybody. As usual he turned on the third milestone and walked on the grass turf. He felt at peace. Last week, '*That*' landed in this precise place. *Chi,* don't think about '*That*'. It was a lie. What I saw was an illusion, that's all! Ah! Forget it; forget it, once for all!

At that time, he heard a *whoosh* noise in the sky. Pattabhi looked up bewildered. The same 'thing'! The same sphere! It rotated by itself and landed about three hundred feet away from him on the green turf. As happened previously, the door opened, a ladder was put down and a 'fountain pen' shaped man climbed down jumping and said, "Hello, man of the earth! Please come here."

Pattabhi, the moment he heard these words, ran away from that place as if possessed by a devil, without a backward glance.

City Tours

Though the boat was fairly big, it could not be called a ship. It was designed for entertainment. Atma waited for Nitya on the top deck of the boat where contented and happy people were sunbathing, loitering aimlessly or enjoying a swim in the mini-square swimming pool. Atma was too excited to read the book which he had in his hand.

He watched Nitya swimming. The speed of the boat could not be felt at all because it was sailing smoothly by the power of the small atomic power unit in its belly.

This trip was one of Atma's long cherished dreams....The boat would reach Chennai in the next quarter of an hour.

Chennai!

His forefathers' land. His grand-dad's, great grand-dad's, great great grand-dad's! Ah! Since how many generations? Their family had an ancestral house in Chennai, erstwhile Madras. What is the name of the place? Ah! I remember now! Triplicane! The computer had given the data as Theradi Street…near the temple. A young man with 'Guide' written on his shirt lapel made small conversation with a pleasant smile, "Are you satisfied with the arrangements?"

Atma nodded his head in assent. The guide was eyeing Nitya diving into the pool like an arrow released from its quiver and said, "Your wife seems to be enjoying this journey." Nitya lifted her head from the water and said, "Atma, why don't you join me?"

Atma nodded his head in the negative. The soft sea breeze caressed his curly hair. He could feel the stirring of happiness bubbling inside him.

"When do we reach Chennai?"

"Another thirteen minutes."

He looked straight ahead. The sea, bordered by the sun, was rippling like a lazy orange curtain. White-coloured birds were flying in cohesion. Atma inhaled the pleasant ozone smell of the air which he liked immensely.

The loud speaker became active.

"Your attention please! Attention please! Dear passengers, attention please! This is the captain of the boat welcoming you all on board who have come eagerly to see Chennai city. This is your boat. You can get everything on this boat. There is nothing which you can't get. This boat is a miracle of modern science. The speed is 500 km per hour. This boat can go on the sea, under the sea and even on sand. All of you have come to see the many different parts of Chennai. For an introduction and more information about Chennai, you may switch on the speakers next to you. Thank you and bye!"

Atma had read all about Chennai. Even then he was eager to hear about Chennai again and again. He clamped the headset to his ears. He could listen to the description of Chennai along with melodious background music.

Though Chennai or Madras was South India's major city, its history began when Tharmala Aiyyappa Nayakan gave permission to Francis Dey on 23 August 1639 to construct Fort St George. Dey arrived in Chennai or

Madras on 20 February 1640 with twenty-five European soldiers and a native named Nagappan, an expert in making firearms. The inner portions of Fort St George were completed on 23 April 1640.

Nitya came out of the swimming pool and tried to listen to what Atma was listening. "Its old name was Madrasa-Pattanam. The origin of this name is not very clear. It might have derived from Matharaju, a king's name of that region or could be a derivation of a seafaring tribe called Marakkal Rayars."

Nitya tickled him. She reduced the volume of the speakers. "How many times can you listen to the history of Chennai? Don't you feel bored? I am fed up!"

"Nitya, this is our city. We are going back home."

"What do you expect to find in your forefathers' house? Do you expect to see your name etched on the wall as 'After three hundred years, Atma will be born in this family'?"

"To begin with, it may be very difficult to locate the house. I wonder what the condition of the house would be! But most of the houses seem to be well-preserved and remain as they were about three hundred years earlier....The tour guide wants to know you better."

"Yes. He was looking at me the whole time."

"How do you know?"

"Whichever direction I turned, he could be seen in that direction."

"Cover yourself properly. You may catch a cold."

"I am hungry."

"You go down and eat something. I'll join you in five minutes after listening to this. By that time we would be reaching Chennai."

Atma put on the headset.

"When Lazarus church was built in Mylapore, they found the gravestone of Manuel Mathra. Mathras was a very influential family at that time. Hence, it is assumed that the city's name might have been derived from 'Mathra'. Madarsa means either a school or college in Persian language. There might have been a very old Mohammedan college. It may be presumed that Madras is a derivation of the word Madarsa. It was later called 'Chennai Patnam' and then became Chennai. There is no controversy about this name. This place was called 'Chennai Patnam' in memory of Tharmala brothers' father, Chennappa Naikar, and became Chennai in the course of time."

All the passengers came to the top deck to have a better view of Chennai as they were nearing it. Atma became excited. He felt that he was going to meet his dear mother.

Atma remembered the hardships that he had to face to undertake this journey. Though on the 7th of Astra he was granted his leave of absence, he had to wait till Nitya's leave was sanctioned and confirmed. As soon as Nitya's leave was sanctioned, he caught a shuttle, rushed to the Space station only to realise that no tickets were available for that day. Hence he was forced to spend two days in the Space station itself which was hanging in mid-air. As soon as he got the tickets, he came to the Earth by the Planetary Space Ship… then changed to the Earth's spaceship…. Since then, he had been spending his time in travels, hotel rooms and strange places meeting new faces which he was not accustomed to.

"Why are you so stubborn? You are spoiling our holidays.We could have travelled to so many new places. Helios is supposed to be heavenly. You and your Chennai! I am fed up with you and your obsession with history."

"If you were not interested in this visit to

Chennai, you could have gone on a holiday on your own."

"Yes. I made a mistake. The Earth is not that interesting."

When Astra came out with the news about the discovery of the Earth, he felt a strong urge to visit the Earth, the land of his forefathers. He felt restless. He saved both money as well as all the leaves of absence he could muster and finally landed on Earth.

When Atma saw the guide, he called him and asked, "Have you seen Chennai city?"

The guide replied with a pleasant smile, "Yes, once per day. It is my job."

"Do you know many parts of the city?"

He replied with an all-knowing smile, "Which part would you like to see? Is it the High Court, Santhome Cathedral, Anna Salai, Kapaleeswarar Temple, Kandaswamy Temple, Fort St George...? Or is it any other place?"

"Do you know Triplicane and are you familiar with that area?"

"Parthasarthy Temple is located there. You can join group 3."

"I would like to see a particular house in Theradi Street."

He said with surprise, "A house?"

"Why are you so surprised?"

Before he could reply, the siren was sounded. "Your attention please! Attention please! Leave the periphery of the boat. Move away from the periphery at once! The boat's roof is closing."

All the people who were in the top deck moved hurriedly to the centre of the boat. They heard a mechanical buzzing sound and saw a see-through plastic sheet covering which moved in a curve and covered the whole of the upper deck.

"Attention please! Attention please! The boat is going into the sea very soon. We will reach Chennai in three minutes. Chennai was swept away by the sea towards the end of the twenty-first century. The old buildings of this ancient city are well-preserved without any algae or dirt with the help of modern chemicals and preservatives. The boat will sink down and travel through Chennai's old streets. You will be given a short history and description about the buildings whenever and wherever required. We will be reaching Fort St George within the next two minutes."

The boat sank into the sea!

The sea was calm and the waves rolled smoothly like molten silver.

Lost my Way

I wanted to see a movie which I had missed in Chennai. My friends insisted that it was a very good movie that was not to be missed at all. The movie was screened successfully for a long time in Chennai and was being screened in one of the suburbs. Hence, I took the suburban train and got down at the station, the identity of which is to remain a secret.

I chased the film following the directions given by my friends. They said, "Walk along the railway tracks, cross the drain at the level crossing, turn at the panchayat office, go straight and after crossing the main market road, you will come to a perfume manufacturing company. The smell is quite strong and heady.

Turn to the left and you will come to a paddy field as close as a stone's throw. But, before that you will see the tent theatre." As the friends said, I saw the theatre.

The theatre had a thatched roof, a single projector, and sold soda and cheap, coloured soft drinks and snacks. I purchased a ticket, went and sat inside the theatre. A dog ran near my legs. The mosquitoes entertained with their songs in my ears. Kanchana, the heroine, smiled in Eastman colour.

This story is not about the movie but about my strange experience on my way back to the station after the movie was over. The movie was fairly long. I was hungry and worried that I may miss the last train back home. I decided to have my dinner at Mambalam station and hurried there.

I thought that I remembered the way to the station or rather that's what I presumed. I don't know whether due to the darkness or the interlacing of the streets, I lost my way. I was walking non-stop but could not locate the station.

I became panicky. I arrived at some market, but it didn't resemble the market that I passed in the evening. I realised that I was walking alone and aimlessly. The shops were closed. In the hotels, the chairs were put upside down on the tables. People were sleeping outside.

I could not find anybody anywhere for guidance. I felt that it was wrong on my part to have come alone. I didn't know which way to go. I felt panic lurking its head within me.

It was my good fortune that I saw a cycle rickshaw a little ahead of me. I observed that he was not pedalling but sliding his rickshaw on the incline of the street. He was humming a popular film song. I stopped and asked him the way to the railway station. He stopped both his rickshaw as well as the song.

In a surprised tone he asked me, "Station?" He looked at me and tried to gauge me by the dim light of the street light. I could not understand anything from the searching look that he gave me.

"Did you come here to go to the station?"

"Why do you ask this question?"

"This is the wrong road to the station."

"Which is the correct road?"

"Go straight. Turn to the left. But, you don't have enough time to reach the station. What is the time now?"

I told him the time.

"You will miss the last train. You can't walk to the station. Come, I will take you by a short route. Get into the rickshaw. Give me twelve annas. I will take you very quickly."

Why twelve annas? I was prepared to pay twelve rupees and got into his rickshaw. He pedalled the rickshaw, turned and took the same route which I had taken. I became suspicious.

I asked him, "Is this the way?" He said, "Ah...aah!" This is how a person can interpret the strange noise that he made.

He left the market and entered a lane. The lane was dark. He continued his film song. He sang the tune only and "*thaana thane thane*" replaced the words. He stopped the song midway and asked me "Are you in a hurry to go?"

I replied, "Yes, but why do you ask?"

He said, "Just like that I asked you" and continued his song.

I became apprehensive. The rickshaw continued on its journey and entered into another lane. I tried to analyse my fear. I didn't know what was going to happen due to the darkness of the lane and also by the godforsaken song.

I remembered that I had about thirty rupees with me which was not much. But what about the wrist watch and the ring? Where is he taking me? I got the answer in a short while. He stopped the rickshaw in front of a house, got down and blew out the light. He said, "Wait here," and knocked gently on the door. The way he knocked gave me the impression that he was hesitant to do so! I heard him calling "Sorna" very softly.

Somebody from inside replied, "Who is it?"

"It is me, Gopalu."

I heard the clinking noise and thought they were anklets. No, it was the clinking noise of bangles, glass bangles.

The door opened with a screeching sound. The hinges of the door needed oil for lubrication. A girl of about twenty stood in the doorway with a hurricane lamp. She had a big black *bindi* and her dress was in disarray.

"So, you have come. I was…." She saw me and immediately lowered her voice and asked him something.

The door was half opened. She told me, "Come this way." "I…" I could not utter any other words. I was speechless. The rickshaw puller said, "You go with her. Don't worry."

I felt that from my getting into that rickshaw, or even prior to that... from the time I came to see the movie alone, this was inevitable. I decided to risk and see what was going to happen!

I followed her into the house. After going through the half-opened door, there was a long passage. She walked towards the door at the end of the passage. She reached the door and waited for me without opening it. I stopped a little away from her with a nagging doubt. She said, "Hurry up," impatiently.

I walked up to her. She waited till I reached her and then opened the door in a trice.

I could feel the cold air on me.

She said, "See, that's the station. Now you go quickly."

Secha

The name R Seshadrinathan was used only in the SSLC book and the passport. We all called him Secha. Sometimes we used to call him Ramanuju and sometimes LBW. The reason being, one, he was very clever in Maths and, two, in cricket whenever he was given LBW, he never agreed. Both our lives crossed each other's three times.

We studied together in Srirangam. We were in the same class but different sections. I was in Sowriraja Iyengar's section and he, KNR section. Even at that time, his poverty was visible. Probably he had a single shirt to wear which he washed every day before wearing it to school. Hence, it had a peculiar musty, yucky odour. He didn't have any slippers and so he walked very carefully in the shade of trees and houses during the hot months of March, April and May. For Diwali, he always had a single sparkler and the cheapest cracker available in the market. As soon as he had played with his crackers which didn't take much time, he used to watch us with a blank look but never wanted to join us in our revellery.

Secha lived across my house in Lower Chithirai Street. It was a small thatched hut. It looked like a book mark between *Sowkar's* (people from Sourashtra settled in the South who generally dealt in money lending business) and *Sirasthar* (government official) Ramu's house. There was a municipal lamp post in front of his house which helped him to study his lessons. Secha lost his father when he was four months old. His father, Ranganatha Iyengar, was in the accounts department in the Golden Rock Railways Maintenance Factory. Secha lived with his widowed mother.

Secha's mother, who received family pension from the railways, was an extremely cautious and careful spender, but even then she was always short of cash towards the end of the month. In times of need she used to come to my grandmother for help which was never turned down. Secha's mother was very fair and she used to wear the traditional widow's saffron-coloured sari without a blouse, sporting the caste mark of red *soornam* on her forehead. Her entertainment was to attend discourses about various saints held at Thondaradippodi Alvar's temple. For her, Secha was her universe, and she knew nothing beyond his welfare. If Secha was delayed even by ten minutes from school, she used to become panicky. If he had to go to the Fort in the neighbouring Trichy town, she used to wait for him at the doorstep till he returned. Whenever she saw me, she used to ask, "Did you study well?" She used to go to river Kaveri in the early mornings before sunrise and come back home in a wet sari with a gleaming metal pot filled with water. Whenever she used to come for a small loan of five or ten rupees, she used to tell my grandmother, "Aunty, I am waiting for Secha to finish his studies and to come up in life so that my problems will be over."

My grandmother's reply was always the same, "Chellam, why do you worry? Secha is very intelligent. He will study well and come up in life."

"Yes. He does study well but always argues

with me. Just yesterday, he threw the plate away saying that he didn't want to eat rice upma. He wants only dosas. How can I afford to buy boiled rice and black gram lentils to make dosa batter every day?"

"Do you want me to talk to him and advise him?"

"No, no. I took the money kept aside to fulfill a vow to Lord Venkateswara of Tirupati and gave him saying that he may go and eat a dosa from Krishna café in South entrance."

Secha's mother was never unduly worried about his studies. He was a student with exceptional intelligence and always topped his class. Since his fourth standard onwards, he was awarded all the merit scholarships as well as all the freeships. On any annual day function, the staff used to get tired of calling out the name R Seshadrinathan for all the cups and medals; all the trust prizes for studies were bagged by him. So, they made him stand in a corner on the podium itself so that it was easier for him to collect all the prizes. He used to get prizes one after another and stood first not only in each and every class, but also topped the school. This trend continued in the college also, and he topped the university and bagged all the prizes.

My grandmother showed her appreciation by saying, "What does your son lack? Let him appear for the IAS exam. He will become a collector without any difficulty."

"No aunty, I am not interested in sending him away from this place. He will get a job in Golden Rock itself in his father's office. He has already applied for an apprenticeship in that organisation. As soon as he gets the job, I will get him married to a girl within the family itself. The girl lives in Adaiyavalanjan. Her name is Nappinai. She is homely and I plan to hold the marriage before April."

Though Secha belonged to the forward community, he scored such high marks that both medical and engineering seats were open for him without asking. I did not know which course he opted for, because I had to leave Srirangam due to circumstances beyond anybody's control. My attention also got diverted and I lost touch with him. In the meanwhile, days flew past with no time to think about my early days in Srirangam. I joined the Civil Aviation Department in Delhi, and was transferred to many places like Allahabad, Mumbai, Kolkata and was finally posted to Chennai. When I was in Chennai,

I was informed of a phone call for me in the control tower. When I answered the phone, a voice said, "Do you remember me Ranga? I am Nathan."

"Nathan?"

"Seshadrinathan, Secha!"

"Secha? What a pleasant surprise! Where are you now? How is your mother? Nobody knows you as Nathan! Sorry! What did you opt for? Engineering, Medical or the IAS?"

"No. None of those things! I am a teacher. I knew that I couldn't leave my mother alone and also that I couldn't leave Trichy. So, I joined BSc Hons, Physics. Now I am an Assistant Professor of Physics," and he named a renowned Christian Institution of the city. He said that he was living in the staff quarters allotted by the institution with his mother. He also mentioned that his mother was very keen to meet me.

"Are you married?"

"Yes, I married for my mother's sake and she is very happy."

The following Sunday, I visited him in his quarters. The quarter was in the college campus itself. It was spacious, well-lit and breezy. I was happy to note that Secha's standard of living had improved. Instead of the dingy street light in front of his house, I saw tube lights which were more than what was required for that quarter. The flat had cots, a Godrej cupboard, and a fourteen inch TV. It was a comfortable flat and he had a beautiful wife. His mother Chellammal had not changed a bit and she remained the same as she was in Srirangam. She treated her daughter-in-law as her own daughter with love, affection and respect. I noticed that Nappinai was in a delicate state, an expectant mother. They had an older child, three years old Ranganathan who gurgled and laughed for everything. Secha played flutist Mali's tape in the tape recorder. I felt happy for him because he had received whatever he deserved. When I was given *adai* with jaggery and butter as snack, I could not help saying, "If marriage means all these good things, then I too am tempted to marry someone." Nappinai blushed at the compliments showered on her.

"Why don't you get married?"

I replied, "First Vatsala is to be married off. Then only I can think about my marriage."

Secha's mother said, "If you say 'yes' now, I will see to it you get married to Nappinai's younger sister Perundevi."

Nappinai intervened and said, "She has

changed her name to Chitra."

I heard that Secha was highly respected in his college and he had got a good scholarship to do his doctorate in the US under the Ford Foundation Grant. I asked him when he was leaving. He said, "How can I go, leaving my mother and wife here all by themselves?"

Chellammal said, "I can take care of everything. Now I have more confidence. I keep telling him to accept the offer, but he is not agreeable. Rangu, is this not a big honour? It seems that he is the only one who has been offered this scholarship in the whole of India. I keep telling him to accept the offer, but...."

I said, "Secha, you can try for a job there. With your qualifications, getting a job would be no problem at all. When you get a job, you can take your mother and family to the US."

"Is there such a possibility?"

"You may get a job in the university itself for your intelligence and competence."

"I, too, am saying the same thing. You accept this assignment. I will stay here with your mother. My younger brother Nachu has offered to come and stay with us for all the help that we may need. Besides, the neighbours are very helpful. To stay alone in this campus is not at all difficult. You can come once a year and your travel expenses are covered."

"But, they have never stayed alone."

I said, "I feel that you are not to miss this offer as well as this opportunity."

Secha said in a careless tone, "If I am going to the US, then I may have to wear a suit."

Nappinai said, "I have never seen him in a suit."

"What about the wedding?"

Nappinai said, "He wore a dhoti for the wedding also. Even for the college, he wears only dhotis. He won't wear a suit. Why don't you convince him to wear a suit?"

"I am planning to wear the traditional form of dhoti with a *tuft* to the college from the next academic session."

"Won't the students make fun of you?"

"No, they don't mind because my lectures are interesting." Secha said this without any pride, but as a matter of fact.

I said, "Aunty, it is not necessary to wear a suit to go to the US."

"I want to see him in a suit. This is my ambition since his childhood. I wanted to see him in his father's suit which was stitched at the time of our marriage. It is made from an expensive material, Alfaka. But it is moth-ridden. He is young. Won't he be interested in wearing fashionable clothes? He behaves as if he has renounced all the worldly pleasures now itself!"

Secha laughed and said, "Oh, no! Nothing of that sort!"

Before I could find out whether Secha went to the US or not, I was temporarily transferred to Hyderabad's Begumpet airport. When I returned after four months, I rang up the college to find out about Secha. I was told that Secha had left for the US. Having first-hand knowledge of his brilliance, I expected to hear the news that Sesha had become very famous and had made a great discovery in the West.

The third time our paths crossed each other's in a strange occurrence. Air India's direct flight from London and New York arrived in Chennai's Meenambakkam airport. At that time, I was on ATC duty. When I went to the arrival lounge to receive my superior who was coming for inspection, KV met me. He was accompanied by Secha's brother-in-law, Nachu. I also saw many college students waiting in the lounge, with sombre expressions. KV called me in haste and asked me whether I was working at the airport and whether I knew anybody in the customs.

"Yes. What do you want?"

"I want to get a consignment cleared at the earliest. This is Nachu, Secha's brother-in-law."

"Is Secha coming by this flight?"

"Yes," he said, and I noticed for the first time that his eyes were tear-stained and moist.

"KV, is Secha not well?"

"Secha's body is arriving by this flight."

I was shocked and screamed, "Oh God! What happened?"

"In the US, he had gone out alone in the unfamiliar New York city. He didn't have much cash in hand. He was mugged because he had very little cash. He was hit on the head and, since it was a grave injury, he died."

"Oh god!"

I saw the casket gliding down slowly from the cargo hold. Both Secha's mother and his wife, who was in advanced stage of pregnancy, were sitting totally shattered as they waited for his body. The child was playing by pulling his mother's hair and was looking at her tear-stained face without understanding what was going on.

I went near them and said, "Chellam aunty, what happened?"

The noise and the confusion in the airport

and the jubilant and noisy welcome given to the foreign dignitary helped to make her weeping noiseless.

As the casket was brought down carefully and slowly, I made a request to Rajaratnam of customs, health officer Sankaramurthy, and the Air India manager to expedite the formalities in clearing the consignment. The big casket would not fit into our ambulance and a part of it was sticking out; each and every one was giving suggestions as to how to load it into the ambulance.

I was thinking about Secha's birth, his brilliance in academics, his going to the US to better his career and status. His ignorance about New York City led to getting mugged and losing his precious blood on New York soil, only to die!

As my thoughts were revolving around Secha, they were debating whether to place the wreaths then and there at the airport itself or wait till the coffin reached the college campus.

"He had written that all of us could go to the US as soon as he gets the green card. What sin had I done in this life to face such a calamity? Secha...Secha...in an unknown country.... Secha, how could you do this? Where is the justice in getting mugged and dying in an alien country among strangers?"

Nappinai was standing close by with glazed and non-seeing eyes. Her hair was dishevelled and she was not conscious of the state of her sari.

The casket was extremely well-packed. There was an instruction manual along with that in a plastic cover. The tools needed to open the casket were also packed along with the instruction manual and the card of the company—'Martin and Company, Embalmers and Funeral Directors'—was also there. There was a card which read, 'Have a Good Die'.

The outer casket was made of aluminium. When it was opened, there was a highly-polished teak box. We could see our reflections on the teak box. To break the seal and to open the lid we had to call a carpenter. Nachu said, "The Indian Association of New York contacted people through the internet, collected the money within a day and bore the full expenses of sending the body home."

"See how well they have packed the body. Whatever you may say, nobody can equal the US."

As soon as the casket was opened, they were struck by the pleasant rose perfume. Secha's body was placed on a velvet bed.

"Come, come and see! Did you not want to see your husband in a suit? See, now he is wearing a suit."

I was shocked and saw Secha's whole body only then. All the harmful fluids were drained out and his body was very fair. They had applied slight rouge on his cheeks and his lips were clipped to give the impression of a smile. His hair was well combed and Secha was wearing a suit of the best quality available!

Sasi is Waiting

The cinema hall was located a little south to the junction between Hailey Road and South End Road. It had a sixteen-feet poster of Sophia Lauren. She was scantily dressed. Kartar Singh was driving the taxi with an eye on the poster. He lost his attention for a split second on her 70 mm cinemascope smile…and failed to notice the man who was in a hurry to cross the road and join the serpentine queue in front of the theatre. The moment he noticed, he hit the brakes in a hurry to avoid colliding with the man. The brakes hydraulic anger reached the tyres, the tyres screeched but too late!

The spectacles of the victim and the transistor in his hand broke into smithereens and flew all over the place. One of his slippers flew away. Ten paisa coins clinked and rolled down the street. With his terylene shirt torn, his forehead, hips, left hand and teeth all badly injured, he was lying in the middle of the road bleeding like a modern art drawn in reddish brown paint.

Such an accident attracts people to gather at the site, but only a few of them know how to handle such a grave crisis. The cars which crossed him stopped in hesitation. They caught hold of Kartar Singh. Some people felt shocked at the amount of blood seen on the road. The crowd, cosmopolitan in nature, felt sad in their mother tongue, be it Punjabi, Hindi, English or whatever it may be. They had a heated discussion about the traffic hazards of Delhi roads.

Just a single person had the presence of mind to make a phone call for an ambulance from a restaurant which was just across the street. Some people tried to shake-up Kartar Singh and thrash him. Fear and remorse in the form of tears could be seen in his eyes. Some people pushed the taxi and damaged it.

The man was still alive. With the grace of God, he was unconscious. But his life was slowly ebbing away. The young man who called for the ambulance did another exemplary thing. He took the purse from the victim's pocket. The diary in the purse revealed the man's identity.

Sasi looked at herself in the mirror and thought to herself shyly, I am beautiful. To look at herself in the mirror, though alone by herself, she felt shy but at the same time, she felt a great urge to do so. Her husband had mentioned that she had a plump waist. She tightened her petticoat. It was painful. So what? The body has to become as soft as I want. She looked at the reflection of her body slowly in privacy, up and down in the six-foot mirror, and compressed her beauty which was uncontrollable within the dress....

No need for any hurry. He will come only by half past five after getting the cinema tickets. What is the time? Half past four! I am pretty. Whom do I resemble? Saira, Sharmila, Sadhana? These cine stars were the heart-throbs of the masses and their names came to her mind and she shook her head saying, 'hmm...'

That day was their first wedding anniversary. What a fantastic year! How many new experiences in this one year! Opening the gate, when love was born, the mistakes, denials, touches, living, thinking, crying, laughing! He... what a great man!

How did I manage one year? How I cried when I left for Delhi after marriage? At that time, mother consoled me saying bluntly, "Don't cry. Anyhow within a year, you will be back home for your delivery." When I told him that, he said, "Sasi, we are civilised. I have no intention of inducing you into maternity immediately at least for the first year! That's my word!"

Nurse Mary, who had the casualty duty in Safdarjung Hospital never liked it. How much blood! How many quarrels, with blows and beatings and thrashings! Drunken cases, police, scooterists, people who had consumed rat poison, people who tried to immolate themselves with kerosene, unable to face the burden of life, people who jumped from rooftops ... How many tragedies! Besides, I don't like the Punjabi intern's lusty looks....

He was brought in at that time. Mary at once realised it was a critical case, 'a multiple emergency'. She recollected the procedures to be carried out as practiced and those which are to be done quickly. Blood on the waist! The pelvic bone must be broken. Will it be necessary to check the ATS reaction? The surgical emergency was to be informed and also Dr Dorai. The blood group had to be checked! The way he was laid on the stretcher did not give any hope of his survival. She asked the person who brought in the patient, "What happened?"

"A taxi hit him at the junction of Hailey Road and South End Road."

"Who are you?"

"I was passing that side. I called the ambulance. Nobody is with him."

"Where are the police?"

"They are outside."

"You be with him. I'll call the emergency ward. Smoking is prohibited inside."

Mary looked at the accident victim again. They had picked up the pieces only!

"Jesus, Jesus...." Then she thought to herself in Malayalam, How badly is he injured! How badly is he injured!

Sasi was day-dreaming lying on her back. She thought Today, Today, non-stop. Enough! Our self-control would come to an end today. Today is our married life's 15th of August, freedom from our self-imposed control... What all are we going to do?

He will come .... After he comes ... then we will go to the film. Sophia Lauren's film is good. Will he be interested in seeing the film? After the film, we will have *khana*.Tandoori *roti*, butter chicken—me, a double sundae and he, a vanilla ice cream. There would be soft music from the record player. Very soft and melodious music! He will dance...cha...cha... cha to the rhythm of the music. Me...me...chi chi chi!

Blood was transfused into his body. Orthopaedic surgeon Dorai looked at the wet X-ray plate which reached him just then. He wiped the perspiration on his forehead. He asked the young man who was standing next to the victim, "Who are you? What is your relationship with the accident victim?"

"I am not related to him. The accident took place near a movie theatre. I just helped him and came with him," he said.

The surgeon said, "The chances of his coming through the crisis are very slim. Too much blood is lost. Inform his people, relatives and bring them here at the earliest. You should have done this earlier. His chances are 60-40... not 40-60."

As soon as he went, the doctor called the

anaesthetist. He asked in quick succession the four different nurses, whether Adrenalin and oxygen cylinders were available. He put the gloves on his hands and mask on his face. He put both his hands up and walked inside and said, "Bring him in." He prayed to God to help the victim.

When the clock struck seven, Sasi felt uncomfortable and the first sign of worry entered her mind. The film was at 6.30 pm. Why had he not come?

Probably he didn't get a bus. But he won't wait. If a bus was not available, he would have come home either by a taxi or an auto rickshaw. Probably he had lost his purse. It had to be that only! Even then, why so late? Could it be that on the way…? No! No! Never!

Never imagine such a thing. He was always very careful while crossing the road. He may even wait for fifteen minutes, but he won't cross… Shall I ring up the office?

He will come! He will definitely come! I'll wait for another 15 minutes.

Dr Dorai screamed in anger. "Is this a hospital or a scrap dealer's shop? How long do you take to fix the oxygen cylinder?"

He knew in his mind, I take out my anger

on all my subordinates due to my helplessness. His life is ebbing out. I am losing the battle against his life. What to do as a last resort? Can I inject the adrenalin directly into the heart? What a hopeless case! How young the victim is!

He died alone among the hospital's chromium, enamel, stainless steel and Savlon's meticulous cleanliness.

Sasi was at a loss and she didn't know what to do! She thought of calling his friend Ramadurai! There was a telephone in the upstairs flat. But…?

The upstairs flat was locked. Sasi felt a chill in the pit of her stomach. I am all alone. My husband has not come back. I don't know what has happened to him. Somebody is coming. I can hear footsteps. No! It is the bathroom tap's dripping noise! Be brave! Count one, two…

One

Two

Eight blood drops.

Chi Stop! Sasi stop! Stop thinking!

Very far away. *Chahunga mein tujhe saanjh savere*…song.

Close by crickets' chirping....

Oh God! I want only him! I don't want anything else. I want neither cinema nor chicken nor food nor comforts. I want him alive. I want him only….

Tak tak!

The noise of boots is positively coming to this house. Let me go to the front door and check.

Nobody was outside. The darkness was so heavy that it could be sliced through with a knife! There was no sign of the moon at all!

What might have happened?

Silence! Deep silence!

She didn't know whether it was after a few eons or just a few seconds….

A man got down from a taxi. The taxi driver came around and saw the meter with the help of a lighted matchstick and folded the flag of the meter. It rang, ting, ting! The passenger paid the driver, opened the gate and slowly approached her.

Sasi switched the light on.

The light didn't burn! Fused bulb!

That's him. Is that him?

"Sasi"

Yes, that's him! I can open the door, open the latch, and open the door!

Sasi was shocked at the sight of her husband standing in the dark.

"How so much of blood on your shirt? What happened? Tell me quickly, tell me!"

"Sasi, I'm coming from the hospital. Wait. Don't interrupt. I'll tell you everything! When I went to buy the tickets for the movie, there was an accident. Don't cry Sasi, listen to me fully. A taxi knocked down a man who was crossing the road just before me. He was very badly hurt. I immediately called an ambulance and admitted the victim in Safdarjung Hospital. Then I found out his address, informed his relatives in their house and am returning home after sending them to the hospital. That's why I'm late. Sasi, when a man is fighting for his precious life, given by God, tell me, which is more important? Is it our happiness and pleasure or a valuable life?"

"No, no!" Sasi said and wept bitterly by leaning on his chest.

Justifications

All the things which I had were new—job, wife, city, including the sacred yellow thread tied on my wrist on my wedding day. Just ten days old and the euphoria of the honeymoon days is over, and now I am forced to find a house on rent in Bangalore. Temporary separation from my newly-wedded wife of ten days. She has too much time at her disposal. Hence, she writes a letter every day without fail which contains just these words, 'Have you found a house? Have you fixed an accommodation? If you delay it, then the inauspicious period will set in and we cannot be together. Have pity on me, the poor orphan,' and so on and so forth.

She? An orphan and poor thing? Hah! What a joke! In Kancheepuram, at her mother's place, she enjoys good home food twice a day prepared by her loving mother without lifting a finger, watches all the new movies released in the theatres and also watches all the programmes on the TV without fail, and has a good time. And she calls herself a 'poor thing!' It is me who has a hard time running after the house brokers to fix a house. But instead of writing all this, I write pages after pages, beginning, 'My darling.' My wife will treasure all these letters. I am at the mercy of the broker Krishnappa, who wears a dirty cap and a coat which has never seen a laundry at any time, pockets filled with papers and a photo of the Mysore maharaja. He wears *dhoti* in the traditional way of the Kannadigas. We both have a language problem also. He speaks only Kannada, whereas I speak Tamil. Even then, he took me around all over Bangalore in a patronising manner with the idea that all the houses in Bangalore were built thinking about me as their occupant. He made me run around Rajaji Nagar, Hosaballi and other areas.

After moving with him for two or three weeks, I came to the conclusion that all the house owners of Bangalore were undoubtedly nothing but dacoits. Krishnappa never grew tired of showing me houses. My wife started writing two letters per day and started crying. I took up writing poems titled 'Loneliness'. The house seemed to be as elusive as a dream in a maze of haze and fog. For the rent and advance which I could offer, no house was available.

At long last, one day Krishnappa came to me at half past eight in the night, and said, "Better hurry up. We have to leave immediately."

"Where to?"

"The rent is two hundred rupees. The advance is also reasonable. There are three rooms and electricity."

"Where?"

"Rajaji Nagar."

I could not believe my ears. There is a catch somewhere. He is showing the house in the night. I have to be on my guard. Even then, what am I going to lose by seeing the house?

The house owner welcomed us with great enthusiasm. It was a two bedroom house but well planned within an area of just 30'x40'. The house was fairly old. One room had mosaic flooring and had cupboards. When I opened the window, I could see the post office just across the street. There was a college slightly away. A grocer was just next door, as well as a wedding hall. What else is required?

I opened the tap and the water gushed out like river Kaveri. I looked up and saw ceiling fans were installed. The kitchen had electricity connection also. There was a small kitchen garden with banana trees and the sacred basil plant.

"The rent?"

"Two hundred rupees."

"Advance?"

"That's your choice."

I couldn't believe this. I said, "Can I ask you something bluntly?"

"You want to know why I am giving such a big house at such a low rent. Is it not so?"

"Yes," I said with a smile.

"I am not bothered about money. I am more interested in good people. I took an instant liking to you the moment I saw you. Many Iranians were willing to pay as much as seven hundred rupees but I turned them down because I am more interested in getting good people as my tenants." To justify his stand, he quoted a verse from *Bhagavad Gita* and explained its meaning.

I opened my cheque book. "No, not today, please! Money is not to be taken after dusk. Let your wife also have a look at the house. I am not in any hurry at all."

"But I am in a hurry to fix a house at the earliest. I don't want to lose this house."

He replied, "I won't go back on my word. I will give this house definitely to you."

As soon as I came out of the house, I thanked Krishnappa. "The house owner is a good man."

"My commission?"

I never imagined setting up a house would involve this many difficulties. I had to run around for a ration card, new gas connection, book a new scooter for commuting and make enquires about getting milk coupons.

When my wife arrived with twelve pieces of luggage, I felt proud for having completed all the formalities successfully. Was this not the time for us to be happy and sing duets like film heroes and heroines? Alas! This euphoria burst into nothing within three days. My wife was waiting for me at the doorstep with a long face.

"What happened?"

"What sort of a house have you chosen?"

"Why? What happened?"

"Don't you have to make proper enquiries about the house before finalising?"

"Why don't you tell me what happened?"

"I don't have to tell you anything at all! You just stand and listen."

"Stand and listen to what and what to ask somebody?"

"No need to ask anybody. Just stand and listen quietly."

Is it somebody's weeping noise? No! A buffalo? No! Or is it the neighbour's harmonium's tuneless music? No. None of these.

"Wait a moment."

In the next instant I was shocked to hear that noise.

"Oh God! No! No! Spare me please. Oh no! Not again. Both my hands and knees are completely gone. At least spare my head please!" The heartrending screams expressed all the anguish felt by the victim. It culminated in a scream which had a mingling of fear as well as severe pain.

"This is what is happening since the morning every few minutes."

"Somebody is being thrashed by somebody. Why bother?"

"*Wah*! Great! What a great discovery. The police station is just behind our house. A person is being beaten black and blue! It seems this noise is heard throughout the year. That is why the previous tenants vacated this house."

"*Aiyyo! Aiyyo!* My knee is broken. Please have mercy on me my Lord."

"Till today we didn't hear this noise! Why to bother about the police station which is at the rear side of the house?"

My wife called another woman who was listening to our conversation near the gate, "Vasundara, come here."

"Vasundara, do you hear the noise every day?"

"No, only when Veerabadraiah is on duty. He thrashes the criminals mercilessly."

"Who is Veerabadraiah?"

"He is the inspector in-charge of this police station. He beats them without any remorse and almost murders them."

"How cruel is he!"

My wife said, "Whether it is Verabadriah or Soorabadriah, I don't care. I can't stand this anymore. The criminal's screams from the thrashings are almost like a cricket commentary about where all the beating is aimed at, be it head or knee or any other part of the body. I can't sleep at night. I can't stand this noise. I will go mad within three days flat."

I remained quiet for some time.

"Don't you have to enquire all these things while looking for a house?"

I replied with irritation mounting, "What do you want me to do?"

"Find another house."

"What? Another house? Hardly a fortnight has passed and again Krishnappa?"

"Oh God! Oh God!"

It was not me who said "Oh God!" These words were carried from the back side of the house.

"Didn't you have to think why such a big house was being given at such a low rent of two hundred rupees?"

"Finished! I am dead. Why do you people beat me here? Oh! No, no! Not the belt, please."

"These are heard only in our house clearly."

Veerabadraiah! The name itself suggests a tall, well-built, moustached man probably not scared of blood.

In the case of a problem with your neighbour, the normal tendency is to make a complaint to the police. But the disturbing noise is coming from the police station! So, where to make the complaint? It was indeed a thought-provoking question!

I went to the back side of the house after my evening snacks and coffee. The police station was in the parallel street and we both shared the same compound wall at the back. It was much higher than the normal compound walls. I climbed on to the rough hard stone meant for washing clothes, peeped into the police station and immediately climbed down.

She asked me, "What is happening there?"

"A man is bleeding from his nose."

I walked to the next street. The entrance to the police station had an arch-shaped name board bearing the words, 'C 3 Police Station'. It was painted in chromosome red paint. There were a few constables and a jeep was standing at the entrance.

Veerabadraiah should be inside. Some men were standing outside with towels on their shoulders. A constable noticed me and asked me, "What do you want?"

I could not muster up enough courage to tell him, "Hey You! What is wrong with you all? Why do you beat people as if they are cattle? Is the criminal not a human being? Don't you have children of your own?" Instead of saying all that I had in my mind, I meekly told him "Nothing", left that place and came home.

I have never ever entered a police station. My only contact with the police was years ago when, as a young boy, I was caught red-handed by a constable for cycling in the night without light. He very kindly removed the air from my cycle forcing me to push it up to my house. I have never had any contact with law and order. I realised that I had no courage to make a complaint against the police.

But as my wife complained, the noise from the police station was unbearable. At times we could hear the screaming in the middle of the night as late as two am. Has this Veerabadraiah no sense at all? How can he beat criminals without bothering about the time, whether it is the morning or the middle of the night, without any respite? You could never ever say, 'Okay, today being Thursday, Veerabadraiah won't beat anybody. We can have a good night's sleep!' But you can hear the screams—day in and day out with no break at all.

Though I have never met Veerabadraiah, I developed a sense of dread and aversion towards him, and it increased day by day. What sort of a man was he? Has he to thrash people without any mercy? Leave alone the normal human nature and humanity, what about basic kindness which is inherent in everybody?

"Nobody has stayed in this house for more than three months. But it is definitely a surprise that they tolerated this for three months!"

"Savithri, be patient. I will definitely do something."

"The only solution is to vacate this house. We cannot fight against the police. These people are in power."

I just replied, "Wait and watch."

Somebody has to take the initiative. If everybody vacates the house and moves away, who will solve the problem? Somebody has to bell the cat! But who is it to be? How to stop this atrocity? I felt that the police had no right to beat the criminals. It is both against the law as well as it is cruel if people who are to enforce the law and order, break it?

I met my lawyer friend Sarathy. He said, "You can't file a case against the police, but you can send a complaint to the superintendent."

'Okay Sarathy, I will do that."

"But there is a risk in this also. Suppose the inspector beats you with a vengeance for no reason at all? This fellow may be transferred. In his place another one may come. The police are a very close knit fraternity and you will definitely face the music. Will you be able to bear that?"

"No. Honestly, I won't be able to bear it."

"Why not send a letter to the editor of the *Express* in a fictitious name? If they publish it, then there would be some ripples and an enquiry would be made."

"What will they do?"

"The beatings won't be stopped but the police station may be shifted to a non-residential area."

My famous letter was published on the 18th of September.

'Dear Sir,

Bangalore police may have many methods to elicit the truth from criminals. But C3 Police Station's methods top the list. Those people who are taken into the police station are beaten mercilessly. Their screaming has woken up many people in the middle of the night in the neighbourhood. The police may not change their methods, but can't the location at least be changed?

Sincerely yours,

Sleepless

JVVerma.

Both JVVerma and I did our SSLC together. Now he is settled in the USA.

On the third evening after the publication of the letter, a policeman came to my house. I felt scared. My wife was scared.

"I told you repeatedly not to write the letter. We should have just vacated the house and moved away quietly."

"Wait. Nobody can prove that the letter was written by me."

The constable snapped at me and said, "Come quickly." I felt that calling Sarathy was a better idea.

I entered the police station for the first time in my life. There was a cycle and a wooden table. The weapons were kept slanting against the wall. There were sharp-edged spear-like bars. They dragged me to the room which was on the left side. I saw a young police officer sitting there. The name board on the table read, JVeerabadraiah. Is he the police officer? What a contrast to my mental image of him!

The inspector might be just twenty-six years old. He was athletic, and both his hair and moustache were well trimmed and smart. His eyes were soft, gentle and kind. His uniform was well starched and smartly ironed. His smile revealed good, healthy, even teeth.

He pointed to the chair in front of him and said, "Take your seat." His baton was shining and he was rolling it in his hand. He gave me a piercing look. The *Express* was spread in front of him. He picked up the paper and read, 'The police may not change their methods, but can't they at least change their location?' and continued, "Be comfortable Mr Verma."

"I am Prakash."

"But you write letters as JP Verma. Is that not so?"

"I didn't write that letter."

"It is written by you only."

"How can you prove that?"

"Don't underestimate the police Mr Prakash. Your house is the only one which can hear the screaming noise from the police station. All the other houses are farther away. A station is just across the street. Your house is at the rear side of the police station. Hence you are the prime suspect of this letter."

"I didn't write this letter."

"The shivering of your hand proves that you are the one who has written this letter. I can prove that by analysing your handwriting."

I started perspiring. I should have typed the letter.

"Don't worry. It is not wrong on your part to have written the letter. We can't take any action against you for the same. Everybody has the right to express their ideas and views in this country. I didn't call you to reprimand you for the letter."

"Then?"

"Mr Prakash, do you hear the screaming in your house every day?"

"Yes. It is very disturbing! How can a person thrash another one to that extent? Such an inhuman act!"

"I fully agree with you, Mister."

"I am not very sure whether the law permits you to beat up another man."

"Definitely, by law, I can't beat a criminal. I fully agree with you."

"But you beat people ignoring the law."

"Yes."

"Don't you feel remorse later for your actions?"

"No, Mr Prakash, I don't beat all criminals but only a few."

"You can't beat anybody. There are laws to punish them."

“Yes, there are laws to punish them. But suppose the punishment by the law is not enough?”

“Are there any such cases?”

“Yes...plenty, Mr Prakash! You just have no idea at all. But I am sorry that the screaming of the prisoners in the lock-up which you hear in your house upsets you. I have asked permission to increase the height of the wall. After a couple of months, you won't hear this much noise. Occasionally you may hear one or two loud screams but you will get used to it as I have become attuned to these screams.”

I just looked at the inspector and stood up to leave the place. What sort of an arrogant brute is he?

“Mr Prakash, before you leave, hear me out. I don't beat all the accused who are brought in but only a few. I'll tell you why I beat them mercilessly. 387, bring Ratnam.”

The constable brought in a dark, rough looking man from the rear side of the police station. His face was swollen due to the severe beating given by the inspector.

“Mr Prakash, I thrashed him last night and I thrashed him really severely and mercilessly.”

I said, “Yes, I heard it very well.” His

screams still rang in my ears.

"Do you know what he did? He stole at the bus stand. That's all. Do you know what he stole? A piece of jewellery—a girl's earring which she was wearing! How did he steal it? By chopping off her ear with a knife!"

"Oh God? Is it so? How can anybody do such a thing?"

"After stealing, he tried to escape by running away, tripped and fell down and was caught by the public. Mr Prakash, he was brought in last night. The ear was bleeding profusely. The ear with the earring was lying all by itself. Would you like to see that?"

He pulled out the drawer in a trice, picked the cut ear and showed it to me. It was swollen and puffed up and had turned black. It had a sparkle in the centre.

"No, no! Please put that inside."

The inspector continued, "The earring is not even a genuine diamond. It is a fake and costs hardly eight rupees. Do you know what the judgement for this crime is? Imprisonment! The culprit would get food at the prescribed time, soap to wash and all the other facilities. Is this punishment enough for the atrocity committed by him? The girl was crying in great pain and shock. How she might have suffered! Why should she suffer? What was her fault? Waiting for the bus or for wearing something sparkling which was worth just eight rupees? Why that punishment for her? How can anybody not be moved by her screaming? Should he not know the pain which he inflicted on her? Is he not to feel the same pain? Am I to spare him lightly? Am I not justified in thrashing him mercilessly? Tell me Mr Prakash!"

Honestly, I didn't have an answer!

The Horse

Some win lottery prizes and become famous. Others are noticed by famous directors even at the bus stand who offer them the chance to work in a feature film, with the launch fixed on the very next astrologically auspicious day. I too became famous only because I was bitten by a horse.

I can see you are surprised reader, and you are asking, 'Horse? Bitten by a horse? Really?' I will tell you the story in detail. First about myself and then about the horse! My name is Krishnaswamy, only everyone calls me Kitchami. You can imagine me in any way in your mind. I am not unique, either in my appearance or in my profession. I am just an ordinary man who drinks coffee every day, reads the newspaper without fail, folds the washed clothes and commutes by bus to reach the office. In short, one of the many human beings who move inch by inch only to disappear without a trace.

I have a wife, a child, a father-in-law. I live in a rented house, am a bathroom singer, am fond of my small garden comprising of one or two potted plants and have a radio to boast about which was bought on EMI. So now you know what a colourless life I lead. That is only till I was bitten by a horse!

The horse was also not famous. He was pulling a cart, which was meant to carry people sandwiched, between our home and Ahmed Store. About halfway in-between there is a hospital and next to the hospital, there is a shop which sells empty bottles and also tender coconuts. Opposite the shop is a stable. You must have noticed, almost every hospital has a stable nearby, usually just across the street. You may have also noticed that stables in any town whether Thennur, Trichy or Bitragunta look similar. They all have the same distinctive tiled roof standing on strong rock pillars. In the centre there is always a plaque with an inscription acknowledging the donation of some wealthy person, say in 1938, 'The water tank was donated by the local Naidu'.

The stable is slow, activity there being almost lethargic, a counterpoint to the city, always busy. The smell from the stable is distinctive, the combination of manure and wet grass makes it so, and the drivers sitting around seem relaxed, almost without worries, another counterpoint to the hospital across the street. Along with the horses, each stable also has some young horses; the foals are frisky and beautiful to observe. All of a sudden as I, and I am sure you have too, while admiring the foals seen them break into a canter and seemingly take over the street, the heavy traffic slowing down, giving way to the beautiful foals.

The stable across from the hospital on the street where I live is just like what I have described. Usually I don't have to go near the stable or the horses, but sometimes when it rains, I have no other option. That day too it rained. So I had to go close to the stable to avoid getting wet. Usually at that time, the horses are busy eating unmindful of passers-by. All the horses at this stable had shoes, all were old and skinny with bones jutting out. It was actually difficult to distinguish them from donkeys.

That day, while I was walking by, nothing seemed different. One of the horses bit my elbow. Suddenly I felt pain and my elbow hurt. As I looked closer, the horse seemed to snigger with his jaws open. Unsure, I looked around; the owner was not around and the pain was excruciating. There was a young boy who was guarding the stable. He too was looking elsewhere and had not seen what the horse had done. I thought of waiting. I muttered "chi". The horse seemed to have lost interest in me and was munching the grass with his head down. But I was scared. Suppose I was bitten again. So I left the place.

In the morning sunlight, I examined the injured elbow. The teeth marks of the horse were clearly visible. Worried, I hurried home, wanting to clean the wound. It was going to need Dettol and antiseptic cream.

My wife was standing outside and she spotted me—the husband who had gone shopping, and was now returning without doing the shopping and with an unexpected horse-bite wound. She fired questions at me. "Why have you returned so soon? Was Ahmed Store shut?" I tried to reply, "No, on my way…."

Before I could finish a sentence, more questions rained on me, "What happened? What is wrong with your hand?"

I replied, "Come inside. I will tell you what happened." Her questions continued, "What happened? Did you fall down?"

I explained, "No, I did not fall. While I was walking by the stable in front of the hospital, one of the horses bit me."

She reacted, "What? A horse?"

"Yes!"

"The horse bit you?"

My father-in-law entered the house at that moment and my wife turned to him and asked, "Dad, do horses bite?"

He replied with his own question, "Whom?"

"Human beings!" The intonation betrayed my wife's feelings.

"Chi, chi, no, no, no way!" her father replied, the repetition testimony to his disbelief.

She clarified, "Well, a horse has bitten your son-in-law, see?"

"Is that so? That's indeed surprising." And turning to me, he asked, "Did you tease the horse?"

"No, Sir. As I was passing by the stable, the

horse just bit me."

"And why did you go to the stable?" Turning to his daughter he asked, "Kalyani, did you ask for a cart?"

"Dad no! I only sent him to Ahmed Store to buy wicks for the kitchen stove." And then she asked me, "Why did you go near the stable and the horse?" And then to her father, "Oh God, I can see the impression of the teeth of the horse. Hope it is not poisonous. Dad, you take a look at the wound."

My father-in-law examined the injured elbow. "The wound has turned blue. Consult Dr Rao. Kalyani take him to the doctor. Was it the tonga's horse?" He looked pensive for a few moments and then replied his own question, "A tonga horse never bites." The way he emphasised the sentence you would think he was an expert and had his doctorate on the subject.

The irritation was visible in my voice as I replied, "The horse did bite me. What am I supposed to do?"

My wife has a good memory and she now began to display it. "Everything will happen to him. He is capable of drowning in ankle-deep water. In Trichy, the Uyyakondan canal..."

Before she could say more, I snapped at her, "Okay, that's enough!"

My wife retorted but this time her voice was feeble, "It is better to consult a doctor."

Looking at the wound, I had to agree with her. It was time to visit a doctor. Only given the reaction of my family, I wondered how to explain the injured elbow to the doctor.

Narahari Rao is our family doctor. At the age of sixty years, he has a booming practice, and when we reached his clinic the waiting area was crowded. This despite it being the morning of a working day! There were small children with their mothers, clerks and men with mufflers round their necks. There was no place to sit.

The clinic itself was small and half of it was partitioned off as the diagnostic centre. We could see the silhouette of the doctor against the backdrop of the opaque partition. When the doctor's helper, a boy, emerged, my wife explained that we needed to see the doctor urgently. Used to these requests, the boy said to her, "Everyone is in a hurry."

Kalyani elaborated, "It is really urgent. See, my husband has been bitten by a horse."

One of the patients in the waiting room

clearly knew my wife. Overhearing she exclaimed, "Kalyani, what did you just say? I don't think I heard you correctly. Did you say bitten by a horse?"

My wife responded, "Yes, aunty. He managed to get bitten by a horse."

The questions now came quickly from different parts of the waiting room.

"Did you say horse?"

"Do you have a horse?"

"Why did he go near a horse?"

Everyone stared at me as if there was something really strange about me.

Dr Rao must have overheard some of the chatter. He now came into the waiting area and asked us to join him, "Come inside Kitchami. Why did you go and tease a horse, that too at your age?"

I explained what had happened. I had not teased a horse. "Doctor, as I was walking on the street towards Ahmed Stores, just opposite the hospital…" I would have explained the rest of the story, but did not get the chance. Kalyani interrupted, "Doctor, do horses have rabid teeth?"

The doctor's response was honest. "I don't know. They may or may not have. Kalyani,

I have been practising in this mill corner for the past thirty years and this is my first case of horse bite."

My wife was now really agitated. "What to do Doctor? He is prone to accidents. When he tried to learn how to ride a scooter, he managed to fall down with the scooter, and this was even before he could take it from its stand. You can see the scar even today."

Doctor Rao examined the wound. He asked me, "Does it hurt?" And without waiting for a reply said, "Wait, I will cauterise the wound." He lit the small spirit burner. Then he picked up a thick book from the shelf and looked for horse and horse bite. "Hmmm... It is not in the text book either. I will give a reference letter to the general hospital and ask them to start a course of rabies injections right now."

"Can't I have the injection here itself?"

"I don't have the serum. Besides, Dr Gopi is better qualified. Only if he suggests the injections, you need to have them. I will discharge you after cauterisation."

He smiled as he worked on me, and said almost to himself, "Horse!"

Then he gave the letter. "I have written to Dr Gopi. Go immediately to the hospital."

As we were walking towards the hospital, a cow was eating a torn vest. Kalyani said to me, and not in jest, "Be careful. I don't want you to get bitten by a cow either."

I retorted, "What are you implying Kalyani? Do you think I wanted to get bitten by a horse? That I somehow organised this?"

"Whether it is done purposely or not, such incidents only happen in our house. Did you not hear what Dr Rao said?"

"I did hear what he said. I am aware that horses do not bite. But this horse did bite me. What am I supposed to do? Do you want me to go and find out why it bit me?"

"No need, the horse may bite you again! And why did you walk on the stable side of the road when you knew the horse bites."

I was upset now, "Do you think I am an idiot? How would I know that that particular horse bites?"

Realising that our squabble was getting the wrong kind of attention, and mindful of the crowd gathering around us, we walked separately from each other.

In the General Hospital, we went looking for Dr Gopinath. Many patients were sitting on a long bench. I was afraid that Kalyani would again ask for priority care for her husband who had been bitten by a horse. Only this time, Kalyani sat down without saying anything. Talking to the patients, we realised that the majority had been bitten by dogs. There were one or two cases of rat and scorpion bites. Most of the chits had dog written on them.

The attendant who was arranging the chits was flummoxed when he read mine. 'Horse Bite' was written on the chit.

A few moments later he called out, "Horse. Who is Krishnaswamy?"

"I am."

"Your chit is wrong. It says horse, please correct it."

"No Sir," I replied, "the chit is correct, quite correct. I was bitten by a horse earlier this morning."

Everyone on the long bench looked at me, surprised and interested. The ward boy immediately went inside and informed Dr Gopinath who called us to his room at once.

"Come inside and sit down. Dr Rao has called me about you just now. So, you are the patient. Where did this horse bite you?"

I misunderstood the question, "In the stable, opposite the hospital."

He shook his head, "I didn't ask you where the horse bit you; I asked which part of the body did the horse bite?"

I pulled up the sleeve of my shirt and showed him the wound.

"Did Dr Rao cauterise the wound?" As he asked he too pulled a book off the shelf.

Kalyani, trying to be helpful told him, "The book doesn't contain horse bite."

"How do you know what it does not contain?" asked Dr Gopinath.

"Dr Rao has already consulted the book, there is no horse bite."

Gopinath turned to me, "Mr Krishnaswamy, I have never treated a horse bite case till now. Why take a risk? Let's start a short course, subcutaneously…."

Kalyani, now alarmed, asked, "Doctor, I hope his life is not in danger?"

"Oh no, chi chi. Nothing like that! Please do not be scared. Mr Krishnaswamy, please observe the horse for the next few days, two or three days at least. We need to know if the horse is well, or dies during the next few days." And then possibly seeing the look on my face, he asked, "You do remember which horse it was that bit you?"

I replied, "Hmmm..." I was doubtful, only I did not want to admit it.

Kalyani asked him, "Why do you want the horse observed for three days?"

"Find out if the horse becomes ill, goes into a frenzy or remains healthy. If the horse remains alive after three days, there is no cause for concern. Please don't be afraid. I will start a course immediately, but only because I do not want to take a risk. Please come every morning around this time. Okay?"

Kalyani was fretting as we emerged from the hospital. "Oh god! What should we do now?"

As soon as we came out, the other patients stopped talking at once. Some of them covered their mouths with their palms and whispered to their neighbour, pointing to me. I could feel them staring, even when my back was turned to them, as if their eyes were boring through. Instinctively I wanted to turn around and acknowledge, "Yes, I was bitten by a horse!" And also ask them, "Why does this matter to you?"

Kalyani suggested that we observe the horse on our way home. I was reluctant. We went to the stable anyway. She wanted me to recall what the horse looked like.

I was doubtful, "Maybe I think it has a white diamond-shaped mark on its forehead."

When we reached the stable, the stalls were empty. Only the boy was there listening to music, his legs dangling in pace with the rhythm.

"Where are the horses?" In response to my question, he replied, "They have all gone out for a ride. Wait a while. They should return soon." And then he asked a question which made both of us anxious. "Have they given the body?"

"Body?" I repeated the word as a question, as if in a daze.

Without waiting for his reply, Kalyani asked me, "What is he saying?"

"How many horses do you have in the stable?"

The boy ignored our questions, and instead asked us quite a few. "Is there an election? Is your election symbol the horse? Do you want horses for a procession? How many horses do you need?"

I explained, "We want to know about one horse only. It has a diamond-shaped scar on its forehead."

The boy immediately recognised the horse and gave us details, "You are talking about Karim Bhai's horse. He will return soon. That horse has gone to the crematorium."

I asked anxiously, "Is that horse alive?"

The boy was puzzled, "Yes, of course the horse is alive. Why would you ask that?"

"Good!" I replied and left the stable with my wife.

Kalyani urged, "Please inquire about the horse every day on your way to the hospital."

Next morning, on my way to the hospital I saw the horse that bit me. The boy, whom I had spoken with, introduced me to the owner. "Karim Bhai, this is the gentleman who was asking about your horse yesterday."

Karim Bhai's eyes were blurred though it was already late morning. He asked, "Sir, you were inquiring about my horse, Sultan. What would you like to know?"

I went closer to the horse Karim Bhai called Sultan. Up close, Sultan, now bereft of saddles, looked much younger. I was quite sure though that this was the horse that had bitten me yesterday. "Bhai, is this horse in good health? Will he be alive for some time?"

Perturbed by the questions, Karim

Bhai countered, "Sir, why do you ask these questions?" I blurted, "Yesterday, that horse bit me and the doctor has asked that I observe it every day to assure myself that the horse is alive and healthy."

Now Karim Bhai was offended. "Sultan bit you? My Sultan would do no such thing!" And he turned to the horse and asked, "Sultan, did you bite Sir?"

The horse simply neighed.

Karim Bhai spoke about the horse addressing more to himself than me. "Do you realise what a great horse this is?" And then he answered his own question, "This is a great horse. It has received prizes in many races. You recall your wins Sultan?" The horse only neighed again.

I told him, "As long as that horse is alive, all is well." And then because I could not help myself, I added, "See, it bit my elbow. Now I have to take an injection every day. Why don't you keep your horse under control?"

Karim Bhai seemed amused, "Do you take rabies injections?" He laughed, and it sounded just like Sultan's neighing. "For what?" he asked. "For horse bite? Look at this," and he showed me his arm.

"Do you know how many times Sultan has bitten me? Particularly when I feed him grass or millets? Did I take any injections?" The answer to that question was so clearly 'No'.

Despite the living evidence, I didn't take any risks. Whenever I visited the hospital, the nurses would tell each other, "The horseman has come." They would call their friends from other wards to line the corridors to look at me, the man who was bitten by a horse.

All of Kalyani's relatives asked about my well-being, well sort of. Their questions revolved around one theme, "Did a horse bite you?"

I ignored everything and continued the treatment without fail. Within a few days the wound healed completely. I was not allowed to forget the incident though. In the process of treatment, I had acquired a new name. "Horse Kitchami".

Kitchami is a fairly common name. There must be umpteen Kitchamis in every city. However, there is only one Horse Kitchami in the whole city, and of that fact I am really proud.

The Sun

Atma came home from his office which was on the ninth floor. His home was on the third floor. Once inside, he walked towards his room smiling at his wife and asking her what she was writing.

She showed him her slate, which had only one word written from left to right and top to bottom, many times. Nithya, Nithya, Nithya, it went on and on. Atma looked at the slate then his wife and asked, "Why do you keep writing your own name?"

"Time pass," was the immediate reply. "I have written my name thousands of times, and after rubbing it from the slate, hundreds of times," Nithya explained to her husband.

"Why don't you read some books?"

In reply to his question, Nithya retorted, "I have read all the thirty books in the library four times each."

Her reply was met with a smile which mirrored doubt and worry and the reply, "Only a few days more." She counter-questioned Atma, "How many days more?"

Diverting her attention, he asked, "Where is Ravi?"

"He has gone to the old man to listen to his stories. You should pay more attention to your son." Nithya replied, managing to end her reply by accusing Atma.

"What did he do?" Atma asked.

"He writes poems," replied Ravi's mother.

Atma straightened the stiffness in his back betraying his concern, though all he asked his wife was, "What? Poems?" His question was seeking more information and insight.

His wife's reply was succinct, "Yes."

"On paper?"

"Yes."

"On government paper?"

"Yes."

"Does anybody know about this?" Atma asked anxiously.

Nithya was defensive, "How do I know? I went to clean his room. I saw this among his toys." She handed a sheet of paper to him.

He saw that it was definitely government paper. Nithya was holding out a sheet that had been given specifically to Atma, after carefully counting them out and numbering each one. There it was, 'Government paper no 32637' on the margin. Also stamped on the margin was, 'Strictly to be used only for prescribed purposes. Those who violate the law shall be prosecuted'.

On the centre of the sheet was written,

Sun, where are you?

Are you Aryan?

Or are you someone else?

Who has seen you?

It was Ravi's, the young son of Nithya and Atma's handwriting.

Sun, Aryan, rhyming… yes it is poetry. Where did he learn the word 'Aryan'?

Nithya replied, "The old man may have taught him." Seeing the worry on Atma's face she asked, "Will this lead to any problems if anyone learns about this?"

Atma nodded and replied, "We could be punished and our rations could be reduced."

He looked at the words on the paper and then asked, "What ink is this? Let me test it in water."

Atma went to the kitchen to test the ink. He was about to dip the paper in water when the warning above the water tap made him hesitate. 'Don't Waste Water. Your Allotment For The Month Is Just 200 Litres'. When the inventory was done at the end of the month they would be caught.

Only he had no other options. He would have to dip the paper in water to test it. Atma made his decision. He could forego having a bath for three days. The difference would be hidden.

Only the writings could not be rubbed out with water. He looked into the medicine chest provided by the government's health department. That department included one doctor and two nurses only. The medicine chest had in it six tablets, half a bottle of syrup and a single sleeping tablet. That was it.

Atma turned to Nithya, "Maybe it will disappear if we apply lemon juice to it."

She replied, "I have not seen a lemon the past 20 years."

He looked at her and exclaimed, "Your

son is so much trouble." And then noticing a change he asked, "Who opened my cupboard?"

Nithya did not reply to the question and instead launched into a defense of her son. "What can he do? For how long can he remain idle? He is fed up. He remains silent, doesn't speak for hours at a time; he stares vacantly with unseeing eyes and now he writes poetry."

Atma was concerned, "Is he unwell? Was he warm? Did he have temperature when you checked?"

Nithya shook her head, "Nothing is wrong with him physically. He is ten years old and you curb all his activities. How can he remain in this hole where there is no place to walk, run, play or roam around; he can't even make a noise. He must want to do so many things, and he can't. He asks me so many questions. It is hard to count each day waiting for release. For him, even more than me! You at least go to another floor for some hours every day. Ravi and I, we sit here in this room only. I have told him all the stories I know and played all the games that I know."

"Nithya, be patient. It is just for a few more days."

"How many more, please tell me, how many more days?"

Atma replied with hesitation, "It is either four or five more years. That is all. Already the virulence of the rays has diminished considerably. Once it is safe, no one will control us. We can walk as far as we want, build a house on the shore of a river and can have a dozen children. Just a few more days!"

Nithya looked at him and responded, "Each and every day seems like a year."

Before Atma could say anything, Ravi came running in and hearing him vocalise the sound of a gun 'bang!' made both parents smile. He was pointing his fingers like a pistol at them, "Dad, I shot you dead before you turned. You better die now."

Atma obeyed saying "Ahhh…" and flopped on the chair pretend-dying for his son. Ravi tested his pulse. The boy was pale his father noticed, the lack of sunlight denied him much needed proteins. Another week and he would get his next protein-enriched cookie. But now, he had to be disciplined.

"How many times have I told you not to write on paper?"

Ravi denied the offense. "No, no. Who wrote on your paper? I did not touch your paper."

"Now you are lying." Ravi saw in Atma's hand the sheet of paper with the words 'Sun, where are you?' in his handwriting.

Ravi felt guilty and yet tried to defend himself, "It was just a single sheet of paper, dad."

"Why don't you write on the slate? If you want to write a song, why don't you tape it?"

"Because it is not a song, it is a poem. There are another hundred lines in my mind."

"How can you use paper to write poems? And what does 'Aryan' mean?"

"I don't know. I wrote that for rhyming."

"Ravi we have limited supply of paper with us. It is needed for vital government work. Each and every sheet is essential."

"What do you need the paper for?"

"I have to draw an important sketch on that. We will then build a machine based on the sketch."

"Why, what will the machine do? What is it useful for?"

"It will help build our future."

"How?"

"Without natural sunlight, we will grow millets. Artificial photosynthesis! When you grow up, you will understand this project."

"Why don't you use the natural sunlight? There is plenty of sunlight above us. I remember you telling me about the sun, that it is like a disc—warm, radiant, beautiful and shining bright above us."

"We can't go to the top on our own."

"Why not Dad?"

"The air is polluted. If we breathe that air, we will die."

"How did the air become polluted?"

Tired of responding, Atma, in an exasperated voice said to his son, "Go and do something else. Now, you will not understand all of this." Then his voice softening, he added, "Sonny, you are not yet ready for that!"

How did the air become toxic? It is due to the heinous crimes committed by our forefathers. The machines they made to make their life easier, the bombs and the bullets.... The inability to maintain cordial relationship with the neighbouring countries! In their desire for supremacy, they waged yet another senseless war, only this one went over the brink leaving the world and its few remaining inhabitants to grapple with a completely different life, after a thermonuclear dance of destruction.

Killer rays had spread all over the world,

slowly carried by air, and slowly all countries and continents had been engulfed. To survive as a species, trenches were dug, deep trenches in the bowels of the earth, with concrete walls. During the nights, the paddy fields with grains of rice would shine due to the impact of radiation. Fruits grew on the land where there were no humans, season after season; mangoes, coconuts, jackfruits but all these would fall to the ground. Only these fruits, like the rice, could not be touched either, due to the Radiation.

Atma heard Ravi calling him "Dad" and in reply he asked, "What is it?"

"I have written a poem on another paper too," admitted Ravi. His confession upset Atma. "Where is it? Where is that paper?"

Nithya and Atma looked all over the house for the second sheet of paper with poetry written on it, only they could not locate it.

Later when Atma reached the supply office, his place of work, there was a note which read the boss wanted to see him.

The young girl, secretary to the boss, gave him a smile in recognition. Her lips are pale, he noticed. She is waiting to get married. Nobody in the building can control her. Everyone is afraid of her. All the same she is a girl, a child-bearing machine. A very essential machine!

Atma looked at the young woman and wondered, do you know what you are worth? Would you smile if you knew your worth?

She said to him, "Wait, the Director is with the Boss."

He waited. Facing him was the blackboard, with all the essential numbers displayed.

'The total number of people: 350. The number of non-polluted, clean cereals on hand, the details about the dead and the living, the expected deductions, 200 grams of rice per person per day, 5 grams of cereals and two tbsp of milk powder.'

At this rate, how many days would they last? Days? There are no longer nights and days. If the light is switched on, it is daytime. If the light is switched off, it is night. How long would the food last? Three years, maybe four! Within that time, something had to be found out. Artificial methods! Artificial pulses, artificial sun, a little of ultraviolet and a little of infrared and a little of white, a mixture of all colours.

Sun, who are you? Atma mused.

The Chief called him, "Atma, come

inside." On the Chief's wall hung a map of the world; it had all the countries of the world painted red. The few circles, which seemed random, indicated the presence of men. There were a few hundreds, maybe a few thousands of men hiding out there in holes. These men could contact each other only through radio transmission. There was one circle in Madagascar, another in Arizona, a third in Iceland. India had just one circle, the hole in which Atma lived with his family and others. Their chamber was under the power station.

"Atma sit down. I saw the proposal you have sent in. How long will it take for the first model to be ready?"

Settling down, Atma replied, "Two years."

"Two years! No, that is a long time."

"We do not have the required materials."

"What do you need?"

"Geiger counter, personal protective equipment and we need the spectroscope. Without it we cannot work on the project. The Spectroscope is above us, in a building that is hardly five miles from us."

"Can it be brought here wearing the PPE? The PPE you have designed exposes the person wearing it to unacceptably high risk. It doesn't protect for more than five minutes. The Geiger counter beeps hysterically. We have to travel to the building, locate the spectroscope and carry it back here. This is not feasible. And it is not possible to cover ten miles in five minutes."

"We have to make a PPE which could withstand a longer duration of radiation."

"Materials? Where do we have the materials? This is a waste of time, energy and money."

"What is a waste? Making the protective gear?"

"Yes!"

"I don't have any other solutions."

"This is important. You have to think of an alternate method."

The Chief was around sixty years old. What was his 'driving force'? 'Project survival?' Some means by which they could remain alive. In the Chief's lifetime?

The Chief let out a deep sigh, "The rogues! They bombed everything and died without a trace. Some damn fools fought with each other and we are forced to live like rats. The Rate Counter is screaming."

When Atma was about to leave, he said, "One more thing… I hope you know how to use the papers."

"Why?"

"Among your technical drawings, I found this paper."

It was Ravi's other poem.

"Sorry, that was my son. He didn't understand."

"You have taught your son much about the sun. Right now we don't need poets. We need just workers. Poetry can be resumed once we have ensured our survival as a species. You should consult a doctor. At this point he is not useful. He needs to understand that our papers are meant to speak only machine language. Explain to your son. How old is he?"

"He just turned ten."

"That is an observant age. Don't punish him, but this must not be repeated again." As Atma was leaving, the Chief called him. "I think your son wants to see the sun. When you go up to service the power plant, take him with you. Show him the sun through the window. He will stop writing poems. And take your wife also with you."

Atma nodded, "Yes, thank you."

Ravi was excited. On the day of the planned visit, he woke up really early and began to pester his parents.

Atma tried to explain, "Ravi, the sun will

rise only after another three hours."

The child persisted, "There may not be space in the lift later. Let's go and wait in line."

His father tried to explain, "Don't worry, they will wait for us. Sleep for a while longer."

The child was too excited. Sometime later they reached the lift. Inside was the warning, "Are you wearing your PPE?"

As it slowly climbed up, Ravi was excited. He jumped up and down, a sight in the white protective gear that covered him from head to toe. His black eyes glowed through the goggles. Nithya looked at him and warned, "Ravi, you have to be really careful. Follow all the instructions. Do not disobey at all."

"Yes mom."

The heavy door opened. They stepped out and shut it securing it with the rotating knob. Then they walked into an iron tunnel which was lit up by an arc light.

Atma gave quick instructions. "Ravi, Nithya, listen. As soon as the door opens, you will see another door in the distance. It is marked out in red. You have to run towards that door, and really fast. It takes about a minute. You need to hold my hand and keep running. Do not look to your right or left."

The door opened. It was early morning. The trees, the rustling of the leaves, the dance of the wind and flowers of different colours... everything shone brightly in the early morning light. They ran. Ravi jumped around in happiness and laughing told his father, "I can run faster than you," and dragged Atma with him.

They had reached the red door. Atma pressed the button; the door opened just enough to let them squeeze through. They entered and saw yet another huge door; this one opened automatically. They could hear the humming sounds of the lone nuclear power plant at work. The machine would last many years.

"Dad, where is the sun?"

"Wait, I will show you."

Atma spoke with the workers on the shift. Ravi waited, his big eyes observing, absorbing. Then Atma climbed the iron ladder carefully and ushered them into the room where he first checked the Geiger counter. Then he pressed the button. A portion of the wall slid away and revealed an eight by eight glass window. The sound of the Geiger counter, "tic, tic, tic" was the only sound in the room. Before the radiation level could reach the danger mark, the door closed on its own. This machine was Atma's brainchild.

Atma told his wife and son, "Quickly, see everything quickly."

Ravi jumped up and down, his happiness complete. Nithya held her husband's hand. They could see the sky, the sea, the seashore et al, in front of them.

The sky had a beautiful dark blue hue, which descended to the place where the sea met the sky and painted it orange. The waves of the sea were bathed in a golden hue. The sun was rising slowly in all its glory and brightness with a chromatic golden colour.

Atma thought about the future. Another day, another date, Ravi will show the same scene to his son.

Atma asked himself, all this is so beautiful, yet we have no access. When will we be able to escape? For how much longer are we going to feed the lie that it is only for a few more days? It is possible that by sharing the cereals available underground, sharing hopes, increasing the population in a controlled manner, day by day, generation to generation...we have to...have to survive another hundred and seventy years?

The door closed on its own!

Yellow Blood

Sunday morning, Murthy brought her home. There wasn't any formal introduction. He merely said, "Ramu, this is Satya. She is going to stay with you for the whole month." Satya looked like a 19-year-old. Her hair was unkempt. All her belongings were held in her knapsack. She neither gave a friendly smile, nor did she frown at me. She was reading a book even as she was standing. "Satya, this is Ramu; you are going to stay with him." The girl said, "Do I have a choice? If you show me my room, I will move into it."

Murthy said, his voice betraying his confusion, "Did you not tell me that your wife had gone to her parents' home for her confinement and needed company?" He continued, "She is a bit strange!"

I took Murthy aside and asked, "Is it fair on your part to do this? Bringing a girl who is frowning, always angry?"

"Why, what is wrong with her?" He responded to my query with his own question.

"Murthy," I asked, "Does she not look strange?"

He looked at me thoughtfully and replied with his own question, "Ramu, how can you make a hasty decision? Have you spoken a single word to her? Why don't you talk to her?"

"Can't you make out from her appearance?" I countered.

"What can you make out?" he queried

I repeated, "She is a bit strange."

Murthy looked at me and cautiously responded, "I can't make out what you mean by strange. I'll ask her to have a good bath." When I didn't say anything in response, he amplified his explanation. "I am in a fix. She came to my house through an exchange programme. And my father-in-law has arrived and he has to have his eye surgery. Though I had earlier agreed to keep her, right now I don't have the time or the place to host her." When I still didn't respond, he blurted, "Ramu, can you not tolerate her for a month? She loves to read and is a voracious reader; she will be no trouble to you."

I looked at her standing there, all the while reading a book. Unable to say no, and reluctant to say yes, I asked, "Who is she?"

He explained, "She is needed for an important government-project experiment. They will be sending her for orientation, before the observation stage begins. You talk to her. Try…she is really intelligent, though she doesn't talk much. And her being in your home will not become an issue. Give her the keys to the room upstairs. She will be there. That's it. She will be no trouble to you at all."

Unable to say 'no', I exclaimed, "She will have to spend a lot of money on soap. We pride ourselves on cleanliness."

Murthy ignored the snide comment and now directly pleaded, "Ramu, please help me now. I will never forget and will repay your kindness."

I responded quickly, "No need. This is nothing between friends." He left saying, "Everything will turn out well."

I saw Murthy off and then asked Satya to come upstairs with me. She followed me, clutching an umbrella in her hand. I showed her to the room. She entered, flopped on the bed and buried herself in her book, the umbrella right next to her. I asked her if she wanted anything, and she replied, "I am hungry."

I thought I was being clever when I asked her, "Would you like our food?" Her reply was matter-of-fact, "Do I have any options?" She waited for me to leave the room and shut the door. As I walked downstairs, I couldn't get the umbrella out of my mind. Why did she need an umbrella? It never rains in our city.

Satya's behaviour was just as Murthy had predicted. She gave no trouble at all. As there was no sound from the upstairs room, it was hard to know if she was there or not. I went upstairs one day. I knocked at the door but got no response. Wondering how anyone could sleep so soundly, I knocked again, more loudly. There was again no response. This time I went in. She was sleeping, only it didn't seem to be a natural sleep. She looked like a corpse, still on the bed, no movement at all. I asked myself, who is this alien?

When she came down the next morning, she didn't acknowledge my existence; there was no greeting, not even a smile. I gave her the newspaper. Instead of reading it, she used it to clean her shoes! And she explained to me, "I am not interested in your news."

Your news? I asked myself, but restraining myself, asked her, "So, is there another newspaper you prefer?"

Her reply was succinct, "I don't want anything."

Not giving up, I changed the subject. "What will you have for breakfast?"

Satya replied, "I don't want anything and I am not eating here again. The canteen will send food which is suitable for me."

I asked her, as much out of curiosity as out of a sense of duty as host, "Tell me, what kind of food do you want?" She replied immediately, "Not necessary." Piqued, I found myself insisting, "Tell me, and I'll arrange the food for you."

All the while I was asking myself, Why won't she tell me what kind of food she likes, her eating habits and what she wants to eat.

I noticed that she was reading *Gödel Escher Bach: an Eternal Golden Braid*, a book written more than a century ago. She continued reading, ignoring me.

Wanting to know more about her, I asked,

"Satya, where are you from?" She clearly did not want to share any information, "I am not from this city."

Reacting to her stalling, I asked her sarcastically, "Are you from an alien planet?"

At this, she lifted her head from the book and looked at me steadily, "I am not bound to answer any personal questions."

There could be no conversation after that. But I continued to think about how different she was. The books she read, the clothes she wore, which covered her arms and legs completely all the time; after all, no one else used the words she did and in quite the same way as she did. What nationality was she? How should I find out?

Her aloofness kindled my curiosity. Wanting to learn more about my guest became an obsession. It got to the stage where I really, really wanted to see her nude. And before you, the reader, question my intention, my interest was only scientific. Is she like us or is she different?

I learnt that she had her bath in the evening after seven pm but before I returned from the office.

My wife had been using the room next to

the washroom as a storage area. Old clothes and dishes that were used only occasionally all found a home there. Normally, I never entered that room. I almost never had entered that room; there had never been any reason to. Now I recalled that there was a door connecting that storage room to the bathroom.

One day, I returned from work earlier than usual. That day, I could hear her singing in the bath; also the sound of the water reached me. I entered the storeroom and walked quietly until I reached the connecting door. Without making a sound, I pushed open the connecting door, not much, just a few inches but enough so that I could see her body. The hot water from the shower was letting off steam, which led to a cloud that partially veiled her body from my eyes. I could see an elbow, a knee, stomach and chest. I started sweating, and not because of the steam. She was not like us. Her body parts were not like our body parts. She was not one of us. I now knew for certain that she was an alien being from some other planet. I closed the door and just stood in the storeroom assimilating what I had seen, trying to understand what it meant.

The sound of the water stopped; she wore her clothes and came to the connecting door of the storeroom and opened it. "I knew that one day such an event would occur. Are you not ashamed? Peeping through the door to watch a girl having her bath?" Without waiting for my reply she continued, "I am forgiving you this one time. Don't do this again. If this happens again, I will inform your supervisor."

I felt ashamed, disgraced in her eyes. And I gave my word that such an activity would not be repeated. Only my curiosity, in truth my obsession with her, did not diminish even after having been disgraced. I just became more circumspect. How could I learn more about this girl from another planet?

Unable to keep all this knowledge to myself, I confided to my friend Thanikai. He had a volley of questions all of which were anchored around one thing. "Ramu, how do you know that she is from another planet?" Thanikai was, and is a sceptic, always asking questions, even if the answer is obvious.

I replied, "I watched her while she was bathing. Her limbs are not like ours." Thanikai was not convinced. "That does not mean she is from another planet. We are all different from each other."

I asked him, "So, how do I prove one way or another?"

Thanikai responded, "A blood test! That is the only sure way to confirm that she is different from us." He even explained how to do it. "You have to slash her and learn whether she bleeds or not."

He brought out a shiny, sharp knife from the shelf and handed it to me with advice. "Don't slash her back, knee or neck. The blade of this knife is very sharp. Pain in any other part of the body will be minimal. You see, this is a laser-edged knife; it slices through the skin softly and is used mainly by surgeons." He placed the knife carefully in a small envelope and handed it over. I hesitated, admitting to him, "I'm scared."

Thanikai was impatient and asked me sarcastically, "Why don't you touch her breast to check if her heart beats. That way, you will learn if there is a heart or a clock inside." Before I could respond, he continued, "It is better to cut her. The bleed will give you all the answers you seek."

"What happens if she screams in fear, and later makes a complaint to the office?"

"Is she likely to complain?" he asked.

I nodded, "Yes, she is a fighter. She created a scene when I watched her bathe through the storeroom door."

Thanikai responded obliquely, "Those who are curious should also have courage. You may want to think of arranging an accident to explain the bleeding or cut her when she is sleeping."

Seeing my hesitation, he offered, "If you want, I can take on the responsibility. You hold her, I will cut her. I won't fail. After all, she is only a girl!"

I refused to go along with his plan, at least immediately. "No, Thanikai. First you speak to her. And then later we can decide about cutting her."

Thanikai smirked but he did agree with my idea.

He came home next day and sat with me watching the news on the television. That evening, the news was focused on another batch of three hundred people who had been given refugee status in the country. The news included a clip of them alighting at the Rocket House and the Mayor receiving them.

Thanikai remarked, "At this rate, their population will only grow and quickly."

I defended the decision, "The flow of refugees is being controlled and we certainly need people to do domestic work also."

At that moment Satya walked in. I introduced them, "Satya, meet my friend Thanikai." She looked at him, showed no emotion and said, "Hello!" and left, walking upstairs to her room.

I called after her, "He has come to speak to you."

She replied while continuing to walk away, "I am sorry. I am not in a mood to talk to anybody, especially strangers."

I was angry and would have responded, only Thanikai gestured asking me to let her go.

Thanikai then spoke to her, "Satya, do you need any help?"

She turned and her eyes grew big; she was interested, "What sort of help?"

"To escape from here," he explained.

"I can't escape from here. I know that you are a spy of the government," she responded.

She was leaving when Thanikai caught hold of her hand. Her haughty manner dissolved. She turned pale and pleaded, "Let go of my hand."

He held on and told her, "I want to see the blood in your body. Are you a human being? What is flowing inside you? Is it blood or any other silicon fluid? I have to check." Then he turned to me and commanded, "Ramu, bring the knife."

Satya pleaded, "Leave me alone. You are hurting me."

Thanikai refused; instead he reasserted his question, "I want to know whether this pain is natural or artificial? I must know."

Satya pleaded, "Please leave me!" I could see her eyes welling up with tears.

He asked, and I wasn't sure if he was asking her, me, or himself. "Are those tears synthetic or are they natural?"

For a second the knife blade flashed and it reflected on her cheeks. "No, don't kill me," she begged.

Thanikai assured her, "No, I am not going to kill you. Just a small cut, a small drop of blood to test you. What is the colour of your blood? Is it red or is it yellow? Is it yellow blood, like of the people of the planet Nora?" He responded to himself, "That is all I want to know."

Satya screamed, "No, no! I will tell you. I am from the earth, I am a human being. My blood is red in colour. I…I came by a refugee ship."

Before she could finish, Thanikai had cut

her and a small droplet of blood escaped from her body. From the cut she received, fell her blood. It was red in colour.

Sacrifice

I missed my flight at Chicago's O'Hare airport. I didn't notice the tuft-haired priest on the next seat. I was reading the news from the small television attached to the chair after putting the coins in the slot. I wondered how to spend the next five hours! I yawned and looked around to find the source of the sandal and camphor smell. I saw the priest sitting on the next seat. An American. But like a religious priest with a tuft. Probably shaving only every Wednesday, wearing a dhoti made of rough cloth woven by hand and worn the traditional Indian way. The thin towel on his torso was worn like a sari. He would have fitted beautifully in the Mannargudi Rajagopala Swamy temple. He gave me a friendly smile. He was reading a very old Sanskrit book which had turned sandy-yellow due to frequent use. He asked me for the time and I replied. He asked me in English, "Are you from Bharat?" He didn't use the word India.

"Yes."

"Name?"

I told him my name. "Your name please."

"I am Mitchelle. That's my previous birth name. Now I am Bharadwajan."

"Iskon movement?"

"No, no. They are all phonies. We have radical thoughts and are extremists going back to the *Vedas*. Being a citizen of Bharat, you would be aware of the richness of the *Vedas—Rig, Daitriyam, Sama, Atharava Veda.*

I said, "It is not *Daitriyam* but *Yajur.*"

He said, "*Daitriyam* is another name for *Yajur Veda.*"

I felt a bit ashamed. "I do not know Sanskrit. I am a computer engineer. I had come to your country for training."

He smiled and said, "I am reading your country's books."

"Surprising! We have to call this a full circle. Vedas and Upanishads are no longer useful to us. You people have taken hold of them."

He looked at me with a smile and said, "You are the losers."

"No, they are not useful for the present day living. You can read, that's all."

"Who says so? In our 'Back to the Vedas' movement, we follow the Vedas in all aspects."

"Not possible."

"How can you say that without studying them?"

"I can vouch from as much as I have read. The Vedas are full of sacrifices and sacrifices alone."

"It is wrong to say that about all the Vedas. Veda means learning, intelligence, knowledge. *Rig Veda* is the various prayer songs of many Gods. *Sama Veda* is about music. *Yajur Veda* is the one that speaks about rules that you mentioned. Even in this, there are two distinct groups, two classifications—*Krishna Yajur*, and *Shukla Yajur*. *Atharva Veda* is all about magic and subjugation rituals. How many chapters has *Rig Veda*? How many hymns?"

The way he started explaining seriously brought a smile to my face. What a strange absurdity! An American priest with a tuft on his head, explaining Vedas to an Indian

Brahmin who had come to America to learn computer science, sitting at O'Hare airport, in the modern age of television viewing at the drop of coins, sitting on fibre chairs.

"It is wrong to say that you cannot perform sacrifices in practice. We, in Vedapuri, perform all the sacrifices mentioned in all the forty chapters of *Vaajasa Neyi Samhita*. We also perform *Agni Hotram* and *Saadhu Masyam*."

"Vedapuri?"

"Yes. It is located forty miles from here. That is our headquarters." He asked me again what the time was. He said, "Another four and a half hours. If you are interested, I will take you there. But only if you are interested."

I thought about it. It was better than being confined in this glass cage. Let me find out what they are actually doing.

"Why do you smile?"

"I am a Brahmin. It is people like me who should perform these rituals in Indian forests. You Americans who belong to the jet age perform these on your soil."

"Wrong. Four types of priests—*Hodha, Ukkadha, Advariyu* and Brahmins came to take part in *Sraudha Yagyas*."

Though his Americanised Sanskrit was

funny, I realized that he was much, much better informed about the Vedas than I. His eyes showed curiosity, the typical American keen interest to learn in detail about things. I didn't want to be caught on the wrong foot. I wanted to know what they were doing. I said, "Okay, I will come."

"Are you willing to take part in our *Purushmedha*?"

I said, "Yes."

He said very happily, "Please come."

We came out of the airport. Since the fog had cleared, ten to fifteen planes were landing on the runway.

I could see rows and rows of cars as far as the eyes could see, till the horizon. He said, "Vedapuri is meant as an escape from all this." His car was parked half a mile away in the eighth slot. It was an ascetic orange in colour and had both BTV and *Om* written on it. Even the seat covers were the same orange. We crawled for some time, then left the expressway and entered into a narrow, deserted and quiet path. I was surprised to see such a pathway in America. The car shook with each and every movement as it entered the forest area. He talked incessantly while driving. They followed the Vedic age for both food and their living. "The ideas of *Vedas* are the best ideas for human civilization. The Big Bang Theory of today is mentioned in the *Rig Veda*. Darkness enveloped by darkness and the great deluge took place and due to penance became a single mass…"

I said, "Our country remains backward and ruined only due to these useless books. If only these books were burnt, we would have been definitely much better placed. What we need from you is not *Vedas* but dollars!" Probably his feelings were hurt. After this he didn't speak at all but drove in silence.

After a little while, we reached a thick forest enclosure, well fenced by strong iron wire mesh. It had a board, 'Welcome to Vedapuri' and '*Suswagatham*' written both in English as well as in Sanskrit. The path narrowed still further and I could see deer leaping around. I could see thatched huts further away. I wondered how they managed to get the palm leaves. We got down and walked. I saw a quadrangular thatched place, where there was an altar in the form of a bird with spread-out wings and a burning fire. A few white-skinned ascetics with red beards were spooning ghee—yes ghee into the smouldering fire and chanting "*Om, Om*."

Bharadwajan said, "*Agni Sayana Kriya*". When I looked up, American ladies in pale yellow saris were standing and five cow's heads were kept in a row in front of them. Vermillion could be seen on their foreheads and the vedic chants had reached a crescendo. He said, "Sacrifice to gods Aswini and Indra." He crossed the place and went to a priest under the shade of a tree and said, "Mahaprabhu, I have brought him."

The ascetic said, "Good, what is the name?" Cat's eyes, red beard. Texas type ascetic. He had a typical ascetic jug with a spout, rudraksha beads around his matted hair tied in a knot on his head. I was confused as to which age and country I had come to.

I said, "Sankaranarayanan."

"Brahmin?"

"Yes."

"Excellent! Pingalai, take him away."

One of the girls came near me with a smile and said, "Come with me."

Since she wore no bra, her juggling breasts were visible, bobbing up and down. It was soothing, whether it was the age of Vedas or computers. Pingalai took me to another place which was open all around, gave me a dhoti and a towel, both red and said, "Wear these."

"Why?"

She said, "Your modern dress is not suitable for the sacrifice."

I said, "Will you help me to change into these?"

"Yes of course, why not?" So saying, she came near me and removed my shirt. As she did so, her body just grazed mine. She put a garland of yellow flowers around my neck and put a slightly elongated vermillion mark on my forehead.

I said, "What sacrifice?"

"Did not Bharadwaj tell you? You can have fruits if you are hungry."

"No, he didn't tell me. What sacrifice?"

"*Purushamedham.*"

"What does it imply?"

She looked up and asked me, "Did not Prajapati tell you?"

"No, but why?"

"There are 184 types of *Purshamedha* sacrifices. What is to take place today is in the 30th chapter of *Yajurveda*. Are you a singer?"

"No, why?"

"Brahmin?"

"Yes."

"Understood. To achieve the status of the best among the priests, they are going to sacrifice you today."

"Wait a minute. What did you say? Human sacrifice?"

"Yes. They are going to sacrifice you. That is what *Purushamedham* involves. *Yajurveda* has rules—sacrifice a soldier for kings, a Sudra (the lowest of the four Hindu castes) for ascetics, a thief for darkness, for lust a prostitute, for heaven a bald-headed man."

I said with a smile, "You must be joking."

"No." She tied my hands at the back and said, "Take him."

Six people came near me.

City

Madurai was the second capital city of the Pandya kings. The 'Madra' seen in antique maps, called 'Madura' in English, 'Medora' by the Greeks is only this Tamil Madurai.

Caldwell's *Grammar Of Comparison*.

Various advertisements in foot-high letters covered the walls. Nizam Lady Tobacco—RK Brassiers—Revolutionary Fire—Gospel Meetings—Hajimoosa Textile Shop (Textile Ocean)—30-09-73, the day the atheists will bear fire-pots.

An ordinary day in Madurai. As usual, the line of pots near the water tap appeared to be doing penance for the people. Small boys were playing in the mud without any worry about tetanus. Pandyan Transport Corporation buses were emitting nationalised diesel smoke. Policemen in starched uniforms, lacking protein nourishment were controlling the chaotic human, as well as the vehicular traffic, moving hither and thither.

The city's human movements resembled a sort of 'Brownian Movement'. A khadi-clad, thin and not very long procession was crawling on the left side of the street abusing the government against the price rise. People barefoot and with folded-up dhotis crowded the frozen tower gateways of Meenakshi Temple and the dried-up Vaigai bridge.

Our story is about a woman who has come to the city today. Valliammal was waiting with her daughter, Pappathi, in the corridor of the OPD at Madurai's General Hospital. The previous day Pappathi had fever. The doctor at the village Primary Health Centre where she was taken frightened her saying, "Rush her to the General Hospital immediately!" She boarded an early morning bus.

Pappathi was on a stretcher. Six doctors crowded around her. She is about twelve years old. Both her nostrils were pierced and the cheap glass stones shone brightly in the hospital light. Her forehead had a streak of sacred ash. She was covered upto her chest revealing her twig-like hands. Pappathi was in a feverish sleep. Her mouth was open.

The Chief doctor examined her by turning her head and lifting the eyelids. He pressed her cheeks with his fingers. The Chief had studied abroad. He was teaching at the post-graduate level. Professor! Those who were with him were his medical students.

"Acute case of Meningitis. Notice the...."

Valliammal was looking at her daughter with anxiety and worry without understanding the conversation among the doctors. Those who were around came one by one and looked through the opthalmoscope into Pappathi's eyes. They tested whether the eyes were moving by flashing the torch light. They jotted down notes.

The Chief said, "Get her admitted."

Valliammal looked at each of them by turn. One of them said, "Look here Mother, this girl has to be admitted in the hospital immediately. Can you see the man sitting over there? Go to him. Where is the chit?"

Valliammal did not have the chit.

"It's alright. He will give you one. You, the old man, come over here."

Valliammal looked at the Chief doctor and asked him, "Sir, will the child be alright?"

"First, you admit her. We will take care. Dr Danasekaran, I myself will attend to this case. See that she is admitted. I have to take my class. When I return, I'll examine her."

He left like a minister with a retinue of followers. Dr Danasekaran instructed Srinivasan, who was present there and then swiftly followed the Chief.

Srinivasan looked at Valliammal.

"Come here Mother. What is your name? Hey! You! Useless fellow! Take out the register."

"Valliammal."

"Patient's name?"

"He is dead."

Srinivasan looked up.

"Patient means the sick person…Who is to be admitted?"

"My daughter."

"What is her name?"

" Valliammal."

"Are you being funny? What is your daughter's name?"

"Pappathi."

"Pappathi. Lord be praised!"

"Take this chit straight to the man sitting on a chair near the staircase. He checks the income. Give this to him."

"The child?"

"Nothing will happen to the child. Let her lie here just like this. Has nobody come with you? You go and come back. Who is Vijayaraghavan?"

Valliammal didn't want to leave Pappathi. The long queue and the smell were nauseating. She felt angry with her dead husband.

She took the chit and went. The chair was empty. The back of the chair was dirty. She showed the chit to the man nearby. He gave the chit a cursory glance and said, "Wait. Let him come," and pointed to the empty chair. Valliammal felt a very strong urge to go back to her daughter. To her unlettered mind, the magnitude of the question whether to wait or go back to her daughter seemed to expand to the size of the universe.

She felt diffident to ask the question, "Will it take a long time?"

The person to assess the income came leisurely after getting his nephew admitted in the hospital. He took his seat. He became brisk after touching his nose three times with snuff and brushing it off with a handkerchief rolled like a rope.

"Look here. Stand in a queue. If you crowd around me like winged white-ants, what can I do?"

Valliammal had to wait for thirty minutes for her turn. Then her chit was pulled from her hands unceremoniously.

"Get the doctor's signature. Doctor's signature is not there at all."

"Where have I to go for that?"

"Where have you come from?"

"From Moonandipatti."

The clerk said *hath* and laughed.

"Moonandipatti! Bring back the chit."

She gave back the chit. He turned it this way and that way like a fan.

"How much does your husband earn?"

"My husband is no more."

"What is your income?"

She stared without any comprehension.

"How many rupees do you earn per month?"

"When I go for harvesting, I am paid in kind with paddy, besides ragi and millets."

"No cash? It's alright. I'll enter as ninety rupees."

“Per month?”

“Don’t be scared. They won’t charge you anything. Look here, take this chit, go straight and then turn left. There will be an arrow mark on the wall. Go to room no 48.”

Valliammal took the chit with both her hands. The directions which the clerk gave confused her simple mind and she roamed all over the hospital like a piece of paper blown about freely in a gust of wind. She was illiterate. The number forty-eight had immediately receded from her memory. She was afraid to go back to the clerk and ask again.

Two patients on a single stretcher, sitting and half reclining with a tube inserted in their noses crossed her. A trolley with sambar-rice filled upto the brim in a wide-mouthed vessel crossed her slowly. White caps were seen. Well-groomed lady doctors in white coats with stethoscopes decorating their necks like a garland were moving around. Policemen, people with coffee tumblers, and nurses were all walking in different directions. They were all in a hurry. It didn’t strike her to stop any one of them and ask for guidance. She had no idea what to ask either. There was a big crowd in front of a nondescript room. A man was collecting many straw-coloured chits just like the one she had. She gave her chit also. He took the chit without paying any attention. Everybody was waiting on the bench outside. Valliammal became anxious about Pappathi. The girl was all alone there. The man who collected the chits called out the names one by one and made them sit in a queue. When Pappathi's turn came he saw the chit, returned it and said, "You brought this here! Take this back. Go straight." Valliammal said, "Sir, I don't know where this place is." He thought for a second, then stopped a man passing by and said, "Amalraj, take this woman to forty-eight."He turned to Valliammal and said, "Follow this man. He is going there."

She had to run after Amalraj to keep pace with him.

There, another crowd was waiting on another bench. Valliammal hadn't eaten since the morning and the smells of the hospital made her dizzy.

She was called after half-an-hour. She entered the room. Two men were sitting facing each other and were writing with a pencil. One of them glanced at her chit. He turned it and looked at it. He held it in a slanting position and peered at it.

"Are you coming from the OPD?"

She couldn't answer this question.

"It is written 'for admission'. Just now there is no vacancy. You come tomorrow morning sharp at half past seven. Is that clear?"

"Where have I to come, sir?"

"Come straight here itself. Is that clear?"

The moment she came out of the room Valliammal's anxiety about her daughter Pappathi, whom she had left unattended for almost an hour and a half greatly increased. She didn't know the way to return to her daughter. All the hospital rooms looked alike. The same man seemed to be sitting again and again in different rooms. One ward had many people with plastered limbs in traction. In another, a row of small children with knitted brows were crying. She was at a loss where to turn in the maze of corridors, machines, patients and doctors.

"Madam," she called a lady doctor and told her from where she had set out. "A group of doctors were discussing. They asked about the income and said no need to pay anything. Madam, I have left my child there."

She followed the way the doctor guided her to find the door to the gate locked. At once, her fear turned into panic. She started weeping. She stood right in the middle of the corridor and shed copious tears. A man asked her to stand aside and weep. Her crying in that place seemed to be the normal occurrence similar to the aseptic smell of the hospital. She walked away saying, "Pappathi! Pappathi! Where will I see you? Where do I go?" She saw a door, somewhere. An exit to go outside the hospital. The gate was open. It was manned only to let people leave the hospital. She remembered having seen it.

She came outside. She recollected that she had walked a long distance from there before entering the hospital through another gate. She remembered the wooden stairs. The chairs occupied by the income assessors were vacant. At last!

But, the gate was closed. She could see Pappathi still lying on the stretcher with her eyes closed.

"Sir, please open the gate. My daughter is there."

"You come sharp at three. Now everything is closed." She pleaded with him in humble tones for ten minutes in vain. Though he spoke Tamil only, she could not make out what he said. She failed to understand his query. He opened the gate to somebody else in exchange of a small consideration which he accepted with great reverence by touching it to his eyes. She barged in against his protests. She lifted her daughter in a tight embrace with relief and sat alone on a bench and cried piteously.

The Chief had a cup of coffee after his lecture for the MD students and went to the ward. He clearly remembered the Meningitis case of the morning. Very recently, he had read about a few new medicines for the disease.

"Where is the Meningitis case I had asked to admit in the morning? Twelve-year-old girl. Where is she?"

"Nobody was admitted today, Doctor."

"What? No admission? I had left specific instructions. Don't you remember, Danasekaran?"

"Yes, I do remember Doctor."

"Paul, go and find out what happened. How could it be missed?"

Paul went straight down and asked the clerks sitting opposite each other.

"What is this? You people send notes, 'admit, admit' just like that. There is no place for a foothold in the ward."

"Respected sir! This is a query from the Chief."

"Are they known to him?"

" May be. How do I know?"

"Twelve-year-old girl didn't come this side at all. Even if somebody else had come, I had asked them all to come tomorrow morning at half past seven. Two or three beds will become vacant by tonight. In case of an emergency, don't you have to inform earlier? Just a simple word that the Chief is interested in the case. Relatives?"

Valliammal didn't know what she was going to do till 7.30 the next morning. The hospital atmosphere frightened her very much. She wondered whether they would let her stay with her daughter. She thought about this for sometime. She gathered Pappathi in both her arms. She held her against her chest, like a small baby of six months, with the head sloping at an incline on the shoulder and hands and legs dangling by the side. She came out of the hospital. She hired a cycle rickshaw and directed him to go to the bus stand.

"What nonsense? Tomorrow morning at 7.30? But the girl will die before that. Dr Danasekaran, you go and check in the OPD.

They will be there. If there is no wretched bed in this ward, there is a bed in our department ward itself. See to it that this is allotted. Quick!"

"Doctor, but that is reserved."

"I don't care. I want that girl admitted now. Right now!"

The Chief had never ever thundered like this before. Frightened beyond belief, Dr Danasekaran, Paul, chief nurse Miranda and everybody ran looking for Valliammal in the OPD.

Is this not a simple fever? Let's go back to Moonandipatti itself. We will consult the village doctor. No need to go to the village hospital. That hospital doctor frightened me and sent me to Madurai. You will get well soon. We will offer the white, sacred, hardened ash ball to the village deity and use the sacred ash which is blessed by recitation of prayers.

The cycle rickshaw was going towards the bus terminus. Valliammal took a vow and prayed that she would offer a handful of coins to Vaideeswaran temple if Pappathi got cured.

The Edge

I decided to kill Vijay. This was not a decision taken on the spur of the moment. I thought and debated about this for many days. This thought kept churning in my mind without respite. I tried to quell it by smoking endless number of cigarettes and crushing them before reaching this decision. I felt greatly relieved after it was taken. The sense of relief was similar to the one which one gets after a good body massage.

There is no hurry at all. I am going to take my own time to think and plan how to kill him. I ponder on why I have chosen to kill Vijay. I don't like him at all. It is as simple as that. There are so many things in this world which I don't like. I don't like him in the least. The reason?

The reason lies in my history. We have to go back to my younger days. The way I grew up, was shaped up, my qualifications, all these will be told to you. Can you listen to me with patience?

Don't call me insane. I am an introvert. Just a simple stare from you is enough for me to get back into my shell and keep my distance. I won't trouble you. If you want a part in murdering Vijay, don't speak. Just listen to me. Don't interfere. Listen to me fully and decide for yourself whether my decision is right or wrong.

First, about me. I am Sarathy. Twenty-eight years old. According to the horoscope, my birth star is Ashwini. Zodiac sign, Aries. When I was three years old, an incident took place which is deeply etched in my memory.

Both my parents are standing facing each other. I stand in between on the bed staring without understanding what is happening. My father is screaming at the top of his voice. The nerves on his neck stand out like wriggling worms. His face is red due to his ferocity. My mother is standing and crying in front of him. I cannot understand the reason. It is just a memory block. I don't understand why this memory is etched in my mind till today. My mind holds many such unrelated blocks like this. Each and every block resembles unconnected islands. These are similar to haemoglobin spots which you see in the blood through a microscope.

Why did my mother cry that day? Why did my father scream like that making his nerves swell up? The next memory about my father is of bamboo. Green bamboos, coconut palm leaves, white sheet, the toes tied with a piece of cloth. Open mouth, unshaved face with small prickly hair, a pot of cold water poured on me, a lone drum, a mud pot with fire held by coir rope, smoke, my mother who was helped up to the street.

Mother didn't cry!

Why?—was another question.

I don't want to burden you by telling you too many of my personal afflictions and be told, "Oh, you poor thing."

Both Vijay and I are working in the same office. I get many opportunities to kill him there. I have not yet decided whether to kill him there or at home. I have to think about this.

In the beginning, Vijay and I were friends. That too, very close friends. I can tell you precisely when we parted ways. What a close friendship we had in the beginning! I have unburdened my inner mental anguish and sought consolation from him. I have confided my dreams to him. My fears, my strange dilemmas and my strong aversion to the many events happening in this world. I have a very strong aversion to people who tell lies. If anybody tells lies intentionally, I feel like slapping them, whether it is my wife or a stranger in the street. I feel terribly agitated when I come across falsehood. Do you know how I have struggled to control this anger? We tell so many lies in our day to day life. A shopkeeper denies having change for five rupees, though he has enough change. Newspapers report untruths. Radio, cinema—all tell lies and nothing but lies. Thinking about this for many days, I doubt whether 'truth' actually exists in this world. All the actions of this world seem to depend on varying degrees of lies only. They say that there is a God. That is the only truth. I had thought that all the other things were false. One day I wrote a letter to God—an inland letter. Don't feel surprised. I posted the letter after writing it. The address:

Respected God

That's all. Is He not omnipresent? Does He require any other address?

I think that letter might have reached Him. What I had written in that is the following:

Every day I have doubts. This happens frequently. Hence, as soon as you receive this letter, send a reply to the following address.

JV Sarathy

No 18, 3rd Stage, 4th Block

West off Chord Road

Bangalore 560040

Writing a letter to God? What rubbish! But I received a reply. Yes, I still possess that reply.

Place: Everything

Time: Always

Dear Mr JVSarathy,

Received your letter. Thank you. Does not the very fact that you have received a reply to your letter prove that I exist? Don't be confused. Blessings.

With love,

God.

Beautiful, well-rounded handwriting. I was satisfied and wondered how I received this letter. I looked at the post office seal, Bangalore-1. Was it not appropriate that the letter reached the head post office?

How appropriately Kamban has declared, "Oh Lord, we take refuge with you."

There is another thing about this letter to God. I will mention it later.

I can't say clearly when this desire to kill sprouted within me. Also, I don't know when I chose Vijay as my prey. Since the past two years, my health has not been good. My losing interest in many things was the first symptom of this disease. Normally, I sleep till half-past-six in the morning. All of a sudden I developed sleeplessness. I used to wake up by three-thirty in the night. There was confusion about where I was. My wife would be lying next to me. Who was she? What was the relationship between us? Was she my co-traveller in the everlasting journey of this human life?

Suddenly I used to feel frightened. What would happen to me after death? When they cremated my body after weeping inconsolably, would my memory alone remain? Oh my God! It is burning. You wretched people! It is burning! Please, pull me out… Fears of this kind. I read books on death for that whole month. Memory is small, tiny chemical and electrical whirls within the mind. When blood stops flowing into the brain, the whirls become dysfunctional. Death is a permanent full stop. After that just plain darkness. A deep cut. That is all. This is the viewpoint of one group of people. Another group says death is a continuing action. It is nothing but casting off your robes, floating in the open space and donning another robe.

By the Christian doctrine, death is waiting for the Last Judgement of God, buried and frozen underground. *Quran* also says the same thing—who is right and who is wrong among them? I cannot understand. I have stopped thinking about this. Since the last few days, I have started looking at my reflection in the mirror. For hours and hours together, at my own reflection. With hesitation, I have started looking at myself in any mirror which I come across without being conscious about it, be it the bathroom mirror or the small square one which is used to comb the hair, or those which you come across occasionally in the streets. Why? I am not a handsome man. My height is only 5 ft 3 inches, that too with my boots on. I only reach up to my forehead in many mirrors.

How can I explain the strangeness of the reflection in the full-length mirror which is entirely different from me? It seems like looking at a stranger. I used to scrutinise it very carefully. Hair, small forehead, thick eyebrows, triangular shaped face, listless eyes, hair which springs untidily, protruding teeth. In the bathroom, climbing up on the stool after shedding all the clothes, I used to examine myself. This body is not mine...somebody else's. Somebody else's clothes given to me temporarily. I thought that the reflection in front of me possessed an entirely different system of its own. I felt that the reflection would remain there even when I moved away.

I suffered from constipation for a few days. For two days my stomach was as heavy as a rock and it got cured only by taking the light brown powder mixed with warm water given by the doctor. Is it possible to take this every day? The trouble started again when I stopped. I wondered whether there was any connection between my mental attitude and this problem. Whenever my mind was vexed, my trouble also made its presence felt. I used to get angry for very minor things and would remain without talking to my wife. For one or two weeks, my answers used to be just monosyllables. When I thought about my wife, at times I could feel the urge rising in me. My mother married me off as soon as I landed a job. It is my mother who brought me up. My father's memory is restricted only to the two reflections which I have mentioned earlier. My mother brought me up by working in various houses, her only ambition being my welfare and my achieving higher goals. She sacrificed good food and new clothes for herself to provide for her son. My eyes become moist when I think about my mother.

Jayalakshmi was chosen by my mother. I used to repeat this again and again to her. I used to tell her that she had to thank my mother for her marriage to me. In the new flush of marriage, why even on my wedding night, I was speaking to her only about my mother. I have spoken to her for hours and hours and days and days together about my mother only. Once she said, "You are obsessed with your mother." I didn't speak to her for a week.

My wife is as tall as me. Her hair is curly and thick but not soft. I have never seen her without the red dot on her forehead.

She is the sixth daughter from a poor family. She used to tuck in her sari and finish all the household work very quickly. Her preparation of *upma* is very different. There are no lumps at all. The cashewnuts shine like gold in the *upma*. It has a special flavour of its own. But it cannot be equated with my mother's. What my mother used to make was a different kind of nectar. After preparing any dish, Jaya would always ask ,"Does it taste like your mother's?" I would shake my head and say, "Another mother is to be born for that."

Both my mother and Jayalakshmi competed with each other in my mind. In this, my wife's winning showed my weakness. My mother stayed with us when we were married. I suffered a lot in those days. My mother used to sleep in the hall while I used to lie down with Jayalakshmi in the bedroom. I used to push Jaya away when she tried to spread herself on me, with a pang of guilt. I felt it was a great sin to indulge in such lowly acts when my mother was sleeping there. Have you read the autobiography of Gandhi? I suffered like that. Then the household work! I used to get angry if I saw my mother sweeping the hall. I used to rebuke her, "Is Jaya not there? Why do you do all the work? Hey Jaya... Do you think this is funny?"

"Your mother only offered to do the sweeping."

"Don't say 'your mother'. She is like a mother to you also."

But she could not think like that at all. It became the root cause of friction between the two of us. When I returned from the office both would be standing in two different corners. I used to stand helplessly between them. I used to pounce upon my wife. She would weep. This happened every day—I used to go and sit in the park, unable to tolerate it. These incidents are narrated to you so that you can understand and observe the reasons for my mind having turned ugly.

Finally, my mother herself found a solution to this dilemma. "Sarathy, I am in good health. I have decided to go and stay in our house in the village as long as my health is good. I'll return when I can't manage. Jayalakshmi is a good girl. But my presence here causes some friction. You have inherited my stubbornness. My leaving this place is good for everybody. When you get a child, I'll return and take care of it. For the present, it is better that I live separately. I am not angry at all. Don't keep on frightening her for no reason at all."

I almost wept while I pleaded with her, "Don't go mother." But she stubbornly refused to stay back.

Her leaving left a void which is not easy

to explain. Why Jaya could not understand an ideal person like my mother? Was she that stupid? Cruel? I was so angry with her that I didn't even bother to register her presence for a whole month. But this wretched physical body! Her breathing could be heard in the darkness next to me. How soft she was! The savage force which exists in this world since time immemorial, setting aside all humane feelings was my downfall.

I used to write letters regularly every week. I visited my mother whenever there was an opportunity. I pleaded with her repeatedly.

"Mother, please come back." She would say March, then April, then May but she would not come.

She left me permanently due to an attack of jaundice. I was unable to control my emotions.

She was gone. I had nobody. My wife could not reach my inner self. This sorrow is one which I will endure till my death. My mother who brought me up single-handedly without a husband. Her death left a deep scar on me. She started appearing in my dreams—almost everyday. Then only the truth struck me—she was not dead, she was within me. When I looked into the mirror, I could see my reflection dissolving into that of my mother.

Then this matter about Vijay. Hey Vijay! My hands are throbbing to kill you. Why? I will tell you. I am not justifying my actions and I am definitely not going to waver from my decision. The fairness and foulness of this action is irrelevant to me.

I met Vijay for the first time six months after my mother's death. The moment I saw him, I liked him. He was holding a cup of coffee and reading the newspaper, sitting at the table.

I said, "I am Sarathy."

"Hello, I am Vijay."

I said, "You are reading the newspaper during office hours!"

"Don't be formal. We are friends. All the work entrusted to me is complete. All the reports are ready. Hence, I am reading. If I have work for eight hours I will work for all eight hours without a break."

"I liked you the moment I saw you."

"Thanks. I have to understand you better to say those same words to you."

"Where is everybody?"

"They all left for lunch a bit earlier, I don't do that."

I sat down saying, "Good habit." We were alone. I looked at Vijay pensively for some time.

"Why do you look at me like that?"

"I was wondering whether I could speak to you about myself."

"That's for you to decide."

"Will you keep this as a secret?"

"I will listen and then decide that."

"Mr Vijay."

"Just Vijay, please!"

"Vijay, of late, my inner thoughts completely overpower me. I no longer have any interest, desire or care for anything in life."

He laughed saying, "Probably indigestion."

"The problem is with my mind, not my stomach."

"Sorry, don't be angry, go ahead."

"Do you want me to tell you from the beginning?"

"Lunch break is half an hour. Tell me what you can before they all return. You can tell me the rest tomorrow."

I confided in him not just that day but for many days. I told him everything from the beginning to the end. My birth, growing up, how my mother brought me up, my marriage, my mother's death, my fears, my thoughts about death, the strange habit of looking into the mirror, loss of patience, no interest in anything, the doubts and fears about not having a child till now! About my wife, the writing of a letter to God. One day, Vijay offered me a lighted cigarette. He inhaled deeply and started thinking.

"You have to meet a doctor, immediately."

"I have already met him and taken medicine for constipation."

"Not that doctor. A psychiatrist—the one who deals with mental disorders.... Wait." He opened the telephone directory, "Mmm... let's see. National Highways, National Industries... National Institute of Mental Health and Neuroscience. Hosur Road, Bangalore—24. Do you know where it is? If you go to LalBagh gate by Double Road, you can locate the Department of Psychiatry. You go there the first thing tomorrow."

"Do you mean to say I am mad?"

"No, I didn't mean that. But you must not get these sort of thoughts—it is abnormal. I feel you are on the edge of something. We are on this side. A deep, bottomless chasm is on the other side. It is better that you meet him before you jump into the chasm. Can I ring him up?"

"No, no... I'll go on my own."

"You can't be trusted. I'll call him. It is best at this stage. Don't be scared. You tell the doctor whatever you have told me. They are all good doctors and are there to help people like you."

I looked at Vijay as he dialled. I was greatly touched by his interest in me! I experienced a new found interest. What he says is right. I needed psychiatric help.

The institute was a separate building by itself. The Bangalore milk dairy across the street reminded me of my mother. I got down from the bus and walked.

Very, very tall trees, long corridor, Clinical Psychology, Neurology, Neurosurgery, Theuro Anaesthesis... How many different departments? How many people? Are all these people insane? But they are behaving normally!

The serene atmosphere of that place made me feel calm. A young doctor asked me, "Doctor's name?"

I had a blank look and said, "This is my first visit. Vijay rang Dr Chandrasekar."

"Dr Vijay?"

"No, Vijay is not a doctor, but my friend."

"Dr Chandrasekar?"

"Yes."

"You want to meet Dr Chandrasekar? Wait, what is your name?"

"Sarathy."

"Age?"

"Thirty."

Short and pointed questions. The form had four sides. He filled it up as I was answering. "What is your trouble?"

"My thoughts!"

"Can you explain in detail?"

"Don't I have to repeat the whole thing again to Dr Chandrsekar?" The man stared at me, tore the sheet with a swift movement and said, "You go straight to room no 86. It is on the first floor."

There was a picture of Eugen Bleuler, the Swiss psychiatrist with a goatee. Dr Chandrasekar was sitting behind the table beside a pristine, white pleated curtain. He had a big nose and penetrating eyes behind flat and broad spectacles. He looked at the card and said in a soft voice, "Sit down Mr Sarathy. Tell me about your trouble."

I said, "Depression, doctor."

He looked at the card again and said,

“Depression is a very general term. Tell me in detail.” He answered the telephone which rang, with a smile. I waited. I wanted to tell him everything. I wondered where to begin.

“Are you confused about how and where to begin? Ok, I’ll ask the questions. You say depression? Where did you read that word?”

“In a book.”

“Which book?”

“A book on psychiatry.”

“Oh! Interesting. Why did you read that book?”

“I was confused about what was happening to me. I had a desire to read all about the mind. I think I suffer from a manic depressive state. Paranoid.”

He smiled and said, “The first thing, throw away all those books. As if your own imagination is not enough! We are the people to read all these books. A layman will get confused unnecessarily. Tell me, do you read anything else other than psychiatry?”

“A bit of theology. A little about philosophy, about God.”

“That’s interesting.” He noted that down. “According to you, who is God?”

“A woman, my mother.”

“Is that so, Mr Sarathy? Can you remember

clearly any one of your recent dreams?"

"You get dreams only when you sleep."

"Don't you sleep at all?"

"My thoughts drive me crazy, doctor."

"What sort of thoughts?"

"The thoughts of ten men."

"Have you read about Chekhov?"

"No, why?"

"He said, 'I dream the dreams of ten men'. Don't you remember even a single one of your dreams?"

"I remember just one."

"Tell me…"

"There is a big bridge, no, a dam. On this side, the water which is harnessed is making ripples. I peep into it. The water is a hundred or hundred and fifty feet deep. There is a road along the embankment of the dam. The parapet wall is as tall as my hip. I walk on the parapet wall instead of the road, balancing just like a circus artist."

"I see, do you get this dream again and again?"

"I can't say. But I remember this dream very clearly."

"Did you ever fall into the water at anytime?"

"No, I keep walking."

"Sarathy, how is your eyesight, your general health?"

"My eyesight is normal. I have got my eyes tested. I suffer from constipation and indigestion frequently."

He opened a book, "What is your impression of this picture?"

"Is this not a Rorschach picture?"

"Don't worry about that. Forget all that you have read in the psychiatry books. What is your impression of this picture?"

I said, "A moustached man is gazing at the sky. On his chest he has two eyes and a nose..."

"This?"

He showed some ink-blotted pictures. I told him whatever I felt. He tested my reflexes and asked me to write, showed different coloured dotted paintings, checked my blood pressure and heart beat. He talked a lot.

"Did you write a letter to God?"

"Yes. I received a reply also, doctor. I am a deeply religious person. I used to go to the temple with my mother. I used to pray and touch with reverence all the nine planets. I used to go to all the temples, Shaiva or Vaihsnava, and also churches. Sometimes I used to feel scared suddenly. Was it wrong to have cremated my mother? I used to feel that she was calling me saying, 'Son I am still alive, don't burn me....' Oh my God! I didn't give her an opportunity to rise and come out. I used to cry the whole night thinking about what I had done...."

I cried.

He admonished, "Mr Sarathy, what is this?"

He waited till I composed myself. "Do you smoke?"

"Occasionally."

"Any drugs?"

"No."

"Who all are in the house?"

"Me and my wife, that's all. No children."

"Does your wife know about your visit to this institution?"

"No. Only Vijay knows."

"Who is Vijay?"

"The one who called you, my friend. He is my colleague in the office."

"Why did you not bring him?"

"He only boosted my confidence and asked me to come here alone."

He prescribed some medicines on a sheet and said, "You take these medicines at night. Can you spend a week here as an in-patient? Is that convenient for you? Where do you stay?"

"Rajaji Nagar."

"Can you come and stay here with your wife."

"Why doctor? Am I mentally unbalanced?"

"No, no! But it is preferable to take a short treatment for a week as an in-patient. Don't be scared. An injection is to be taken daily. That is all.

"Insulin shock?"

"Look here, I have already told you to forget all that you have read. But you have to spend a week here definitely. Preferably, get admitted tomorrow itself."

"Why don't you prescribe the injection? I'll get it injected by a doctor nearby."

"It's not like that. The reaction is to be observed. It's better that you remain as an in-patient. Will you come?"

"These tablets?"

"Just plain sleeping tablets. You might have taken some on your own."

"I have taken only some tranquilizers. Librium..."

"Just leave out everything. Come tomorrow at the same time. Okay? There is nothing wrong with you. You are alright."

"Doctor, why don't you say that I am normal?"

"Alright, normal! Can you bring the reply from God when you come tomorrow?"

"Definitely."

As I was returning by auto rickshaw, I thought deeply about the doctor's reaction to me. If I am normal, why admit me as an in-patient in a mental hospital? Why an injection every day? I had spoken a lot with him. Was there anything wrong with what I had said? No, probably he detected something wrong with my mental equilibrium, hence, I needed some psychiatric treatment. What the heck! It was wrong to have gone there. Now how do I tell this to my wife? If I have to get admitted in the mental hospital tomorrow, she will start imagining things...

These specialists are rotten. Rascals. What is wrong if the injection can be arranged at home. This proves the injection is not an ordinary one. Shock...electric? No, but some strong anaesthetic medicines. No, I am not going there. What is wrong with me? Nothing. My mother is alive. She will be reborn as my child. She is going to take divine incarnation. If I can't get her through my wife, I'll force all other women and get her through one of them.

This is a divine secret.

Vijay met me during the lunch break. He asked, "Did you go?"

"Mmm..."

"What did he say? He is supposed to be a renowned doctor."

"The doctor said that I have to get admitted in the hospital."

"Good. Fine. Take leave of absence. Get admitted and be relaxed."

"I am not going there."

"Why?"

"Nothing is wrong with me. He said I was normal."

"Then why did he suggest that you get admitted?"

"Why, you tell me."

"Sarathy! Don't be stubborn. He knows what he is talking about. Why don't you listen to him?"

"I am definitely not going."

"Don't be stupid."

"He is stupid. Why should he ask a normal person to get admitted?"

"He might have said normal without meaning it so that you won't feel scared. You are not normal."

"Then why would the doctor tell a lie? I don't like lies."

Vijay got angry. "Look, something is definitely terribly wrong with you. He alone can treat you. You must go there positively."

"Jaya will be scared."

"I'll tell her, convince her."

"Who are you to talk to my wife?"

"There you go again." Vijay's hands trembled. He filled a glass with water and drank. I left the place.

"Sarathy, don't go. I have to tell you something."

"What is it?"

"I am worried about you, Sarathy! Do you remember the letter that you wrote to God?"

"Yes. The doctor has asked me to bring the reply."

"Do you know who wrote the reply? Me. You idiot, it was only me. As if God will reply to any letter. That was my handwriting...."

I was shocked and said, "You wretch."

"Listen to this also. Do you remember what all you have told me about yourself? Probably you don't remember anything. The thoughts of your younger days, the way your mother brought you up, your neighbours... Did you say all this to the doctor?"

"Mmm..."

"From all the incidents that you have narrated, one thing is very clear to me. Have you noticed that?"

"What is it?"

"Shall I tell you? Can you bear it?"

"Say it! Say it! I am normal. I can bear anything."

"The way your mother lived! My dear Sarathy, kindle your memories again. Dig out the thought which is deeply embedded in your memory. You were mentioning Raju. Who is Raju? Why did he visit every week? Sarathy, try and recollect clearly. The toy monkey which walked when wound. The toy which hopped, making a *chirk chirk* noise. Who gave you that? Raju uncle! You played with it always. You lost it one day and went looking for it. You went into the bedroom quietly without making any noise. What did you see?"

I closed my ears. "Oh God! Don't say anything. Don't say anything. I didn't see anything. Stop Vijay, stop."

"From where did you get the money for your education? How did you get the new boots? How did the money come to the hostel every month regularly without fail? How Sarathy? How?"

"Don't say anything. Stop! Stop! What you say is absolute rubbish and nonsense. Please Vijay, don't speak any further. Stop! Don't confuse me. Don't spoil the only perfect picture within me. You are an evil person with perverted ideas. That's why you are thinking like this."

He laughed saying, "I am speaking the truth...Then on Ram Navami day…."

"Are you going to stop now or shall I kill you?"

"Look Sarathy, you can kill me, but you can't kill your thoughts. Go. Go back home! Go to the hospital tomorrow positively. Launder all your thoughts clean. Make your mind like a pristine white curtain. Destroy all the red Rorschach pictures. Search for peace. Hurry up! Take leave of absence and run!"

I ran. Vijay's mocking laughter could be heard inside my head. All that he said was lies. What sort of a perverted person is he? Trying to poison my mind by narrating this sort of gossip. What sort of sadist is he? Is there any truth in what he says? He is just blabbering. Cruel man! The wretch! Pervert! I should not have spoken to him at all. How bad a person is he to imply such perverted ideas! He wants to destroy me completely. My telling him about the letter to God and his ridiculing me by sending a reply to it reveals his true nature as a mean person. Dr Chandrasekar had his doubts about my mental balance when he was informed about the letter. I don't want anything to do with Vijay at all. I don't want to talk to him at all. No need to have a smoke or coffee in his company. But what to do with him? How can I let him live after the way he has slandered my mother? I have to finish him off. I should have strangled him to death then and there itself! Wait, Wait! Think calmly. No need for any hurry. I have to kill him by planning meticulously. Be patient and cautious.

I came home. Jaya woke up from her afternoon nap. She looked at me fearfully and asked, "Why have you come early, are you not well?"

I said, "I'm okay." I went straight into the bathroom. I looked at my face in the bathroom mirror for a few minutes. My face changed. First the moustache and the beard grew, eyes sank deep into their sockets and shrunk into the skull only to transform into a flaxen-haired baby with chubby cheeks and lovely eyes, full of life....

Mother! This is my duty. I have to do this. This slaying is essential to establish the principles as well as the truth I firmly believe in. To destroy falsehood, the only option left for me is to kill Vijay.

Jaya knocked on the bathroom door.

Be careful. Nobody is to know about my decision. I have to behave like a normal person to the outside world. I opened the door after washing and wiping my face with a towel. I said, "What is it?"

"Thank god. I was scared. What is the matter? Why were you perspiring so profusely?"

"There's nothing wrong with me, Jaya. Can I have a cup of coffee?"

"I'll make it just now."

"Come, let's go to the cinema and be happy."

She looked at me as if seeing me for the first time.

"Jaya! Have I not acted strangely with you many times?"

"You treat me any way you like, but please talk to me. What tortures me the most is when you sit quietly for hours and hours, and days and days without talking."

"I won't behave like that again, Jaya. We can have coffee outside. Just get dressed."

She ran inside with new-found happiness.

How am I different from the others? I behaved just like any normal husband. I walked with her upto the bus stand, gave up the one available seat to her and got the tickets. I stood in the queue at the cinema for balcony seats, purchased popcorn for her, enjoyed all the advertisements shown on the screen.... How could I be called abnormal? That rascal doctor is telling lies. Vijay... I don't want to think about that wretched sinner!

The film was all about love. The music was loud and noisy. At one stage, my attention was diverted from the film. I saw the Rorschach picture playing on the screen. I closed my eyes.

She shook me saying, "Don't you like the film? Shall we go?"

I said, "No." It was intermission. I went to the restroom. I looked at the mirror and was shocked to see Vijay standing in the queue. I turned around and pretended that I hadn't seen him. He had come on his own.

He said, " Hello, Sarathy."

I didn't answer him. What is this, why

won't he leave me alone?

"Are you angry with me because I asked you that question?"

I didn't answer him.

"I thought about it after you left. Sarathy, it was wrong on my part to have said those things. I felt very bad afterwards. I could not work in the office. I left after taking permission. I just entered the theatre to see this film. It was my good fortune that I saw you here so that I could apologize to you."

I didn't answer him at all.

"Sarathy, will you never ever talk to me?"

How dare he? He has destroyed my mind completely. Planted a poisonous seed within it and now asks me why I am angry with him and whether I will talk to him. Vijay! Yes, I am angry. You are going to be punished for your action. Death sentence—beware.

When I returned to my seat, the film had begun. A film started in my mind also. My mind too replayed the visuals uttered by him in the morning. The words transformed themselves into colours, first black then a dirty brown and started oozing out all over my mind. In a corner of my mind, a devil peeped out and wondered whether there could be any truth in what he said. The other part said that it was very wrong even to think like that. My wife synchronized with the celluloid figures and cried, laughed and shuddered. I also cried, laughed and shuddered in my own personal film.

We had coffee and snacks in a hotel in Ananda Rao circle. My wife was very happy. She said, "Please remain like this always."

Days! How many more days are left to kill Vijjayan? Then? I will be arrested.

Death sentence? Life imprisonment?

She said, "Can I ask you something?"

"What is it?"

"Somebody from your office said something."

I was alarmed and asked, "Who and what?"

"Natesan."

Thank God! It's Natesan and not Vijay. I sighed in relief. "What did he say?" "People in your office are going to Nandi Hills for a picnic this coming Saturday."

"Yes, so?"

"Can we join them?" I felt a sense of elation all of a sudden. Picnic! Nandi Hill! Vijay also would be there. Yes. There I'd get many opportunities to finish him off. "Jaya, a good idea. We will definitely go. I will ask them to include our names also tomorrow itself. We have not gone on a picnic like this, happily, since a long time...." She pressed my hand joyfully. I was thinking about Nandi Hills as we were returning home. I had been there once about five years back. A tall hill... a big bungalow. A lone hotel. Tipu's drop. The peak which slopes down suddenly to a deep gorge. I felt happy. An unexpected opportunity given by God. Though he didn't reply to my letter with his own hands, he has answered me indirectly. He has proved his presence by arranging this favourable situation. Oh God, you are definitely great! I could not sleep that night even after taking the tablets. Vijay's words were reverberating in my mind. "How did you get the money for your education? How did you get the new boots? How did you get money in the hostel regularly, without fail? Sarathy, how?"

"Don't say anything. Stop, Stop!"

"I'll definitely say these things. I'll repeat again and again. Shall I ask you something? That day you returned home failing to get a ticket for the film!"

"No, please don't say anything I beg of you."

My wife shook me to wakefulness. "What happened? Did you have an unpleasant dream?"

"No!"

"Here, have some water."

I could have no peace of mind as long as Vijay was alive, even if I remained without talking to him till the end of my days! Just seeing him makes me lose my patience. How dared he, the scoundrel? What right had he to talk like this? No, he has to die definitely. I have to kill him first before I do anything else. Dear Nandi Hills, here I come. Oh my dear hills, you are going to liberate me, I'm coming. I have decided to kill him, definitely! All my mental torture will end when Vijay is finished. Is it necessary that I will be caught? I can escape if I plan meticulously. The plan is to be executed with a lot of deliberation, and without anybody suspecting me.

My conscience is not going to prick me after I kill Vijay. I am not going to feel guilty at all. He is the devil who possessed me and rattled my mind. I'll be happy thinking 'good riddance'. I do not need a doctor, or injections or medicines of any sort. Vijay has to be finished off. I'll finish him off.

Later, I slept peacefully.

The next day, the moment I reached the office, I gave both my name as well as my wife's for the picnic. Then I told Natesan casually, "Natesan, let me have a look at the list of names."

"Why?"

"Just to have an idea who all are coming."

I saw the list. Vijay's name was also there. Thank God! I returned to my seat. Will Natesan remember what I asked him just now? No, No! Don't feel scared. What is wrong in asking who all are coming on the trip? That's a natural query. Sarathy don't be scared, don't be scared.

Vijay again came to me in the afternoon. I pretended to be engrossed in my files and ignored him.

"What? Still angry with me?"

I didn't answer.

"When will you talk to me? At least let me know that."

I stared at him, with fire in my eyes.

He laughed and said, "You may burn me to death by that look, Sarathy. People tend to get angry when the truth is told."

"Get out."

"I'll leave. But think about what I said in a

calm manner. Even now, it is not too late. You may go to the doctor tomorrow. He will tell you what is best for you. He will erase everything."

"Vijay, I am definitely going to erase everything."

"You seem to have given your name for the picnic...very good. Will you talk to me there at least or are you going to sulk? Will you introduce your wife to me?" Saying this, he laughed.

I am going to introduce you to something, but not my wife.

We left for Nandi Hills at nine in the morning. Thirty-five people from the office had come. Everyone was happy. Transistors were blaring. I too was a part of the childish exuberance but only superficially. My wife brought a lot of eatables—rice mixed with spices, chocolates, cookies, coffee, juice. I was sitting next to her. Vijay was sitting next to me by the window and looking outside.

Many hallis like Kanganahalli, Devanahalli passed us and I browsed through the newspaper. An article titled *Independence* caught my attention.

'We lose our independence the moment we are born. The place we are born, country, family, parents, wife are all decided at that time itself, hence, where is the independence?'

Vijay said, "What are you reading?"

"Can't you see?"

"Thank God you have spoken."

"Wait, I'm going to speak Vijay, I'm going to speak a lot."

My wife was talking to me non-stop. "Looking back, it is five years since we have gone anywhere like this. Thank heavens! It is almost two years since we have spoken to each other with such gay abandon."

Jaya, how am I to tell you that this is the last day for you to talk to me with so much happiness? How will she face the news that her husband committed a murder? Who is going to catch me? I am going to execute this after planning meticulously so that nobody will suspect me. I said, "Jaya, don't worry I will always talk to you much more and also happily."

Her face caressed my shoulder as she leaned against me. Vijay gazed outside.

The two humps of Nandi Hills could be seen at a distance. The bus strained to climb up. 'Hair pin bends', 'sound horn', 'no overtaking', 3,800 feet, 4,000 feet. We reached the entrance to Tipu Sultan's fort. Tickets were purchased. Some people had tender coconut water. "Jaya, do you want a coconut?" For a split second, the paring of the coconut reminded me of Vijay's head.

A school bus with children in uniform came and halted there. The children were happy and made a lot of noise. All of us climbed up the stairs talking among ourselves. Plenty of shaded slopes, short trees which seemed to invite even old people to climb them. The horse stables of Sultan's days, canon holes ... a statue of a bull right in the middle, a hotel with glass windows at the peak of the hill with fantastic views, Gabban House. An antique temple.

A traditional picnic on thick sheets spread out under the shade of the trees...eating heartily...playing cards...laughing...chasing each other...dancing to the music...playing and singing.

Lowly people! Mean people! Me? I'm great! I am going to execute a great deed from a great height!

I said, "Vijay, I want to speak to you, alone." He looked at me and said, "Thank God! The ice is broken. Speak to me."

"No, not here, but alone. Can you come with me?"

"By all means."

"Jaya, you take rest here. I am going to walk with my friend for a while."

"What, let her also come."

"No, Jaya, you stay here. You can see everyone playing some games. Join them."

Vijay smiled. "You want me to come alone with you. You want to tell me something. You are very angry. Is that so?"

"No, no."

We both walked along the gently sloping steps. We were quiet for sometime.

"What is this, why are you not talking?"

"Vijay, I thought about what you said."

"What did I say?"

"The doubt which you pointed out. It is deeply embedded in my mind like a poisonous seed. I need your help to pluck it out. I have lost my sleep. I am completely swallowed up by that disastrous incident."

"That is precisely why I suggested a remedy for it. Get yourself admitted in the hospital. They will send you back after thoroughly cleaning you."

"No, I have thought of a different method."

"There is no other alternative method for this."

"Yes, there is another one positively, Vijay."

"What is it?"

"Don't be in a hurry, come with me…"

We climed up. Jacaranda trees were in full bloom with mauve flowers, sans leaves. I asked a passer-by, "Where is Tipu's drop?"

He answered, "Go straight." We climbed down the incline slowly.

"Where are we going?"

"To an excellent place to speak in confidence."

I had made up my mind. Tipu's Drop was an unexpectedly steep incline. The place designated by the Sultan to punish the guilty. That's where I am going to kill him.

We climbed down carefully. The hill supported the fort wall. It had a semi-circular ring with waist-high square cuts. I went there and peeped out. Down below I could see the road resembling a green vein. There was a sloping rock with a perpendicular fall of a thousand feet. My feet felt an itching sensation. I sat in between the edges. The breeze gently kissed me. "Vijay, look. What a beautiful place. Come and sit here beside me."

He sat with some hesitation.

"Did you bring me here to speak about the beauty of nature?"

Many scribbles could be seen on the lime mortared walls—names and numbers. Everybody wants to mark their names. A small place in history, including me.

"Vijay, look at this open space. Look below. Feel the air. How pure it is. Look at the village which is far below.... The houses look like toy houses, human beings resemble just plain dots... cars wriggle like worms.... From this elevated height, it is obvious that human life is nothing but just a speck. Even in that speck, there are distinctions like good and bad, virtuous and sinful deeds. We have to give up everything to purify all the sinful and evil thoughts arising in our mind. You too wash your dirty feelings in this open space. Come Vijay!"

"What are you saying?"

"Vijay, I'll tell you clearly in simple words. You have planted a thorn in my mind. The only way for me to remove the thorn is to kill you. Your death alone will wipe out the thought. Otherwise, whenever I see you, I will be reminded of the doubt which you have sown within me. I can't possibly live with that fire raging within my mind. So you have to die."

"Hey Sarathy! what is this? What are you blabbering?"

"Vijay, this is the punishment awarded to you by me in my private court, under special jurisdiction. Get lost, you devil!"

I held him tightly and made him climb up along with me to the edge.

"Hey you! Hey Sarathy! Please think again. What you are doing is wrong. Whatever I said was all in jest. No Sarathy, leave me. Hey! leave me."

"No Vijay, you have to die. This moment was already predetermined when you were born."

He held onto me with a strong, vice-like grip. "Sarathy, no, I am scared. Please."

"Nothing will happen. A swim in the big open space. Then a single breaking sound. You will die within a second. Before your mind can register the pain, your brain will be smashed to pieces. Don't be afraid. Goodbye Vijay." In a violent fit of rage, I shook him and pushed him away from me.

"Oh my God! What is this? The rascal has dragged me also down with him. Hey Vijay let go of me! You fool, you have avenged me." Both Vijay and I fell into the deep gorge, stuck together. I could hear the hissing sound of the air around me...second by second, the earth was in a hurry to meet us. I don't know whether the blood gushed into my brain but we both fell very very quickly.

PS Nandi Hills police outpost received a message, transmitted by a VHF radio from a small room near the temple on the hill. A police jeep arrived and people who had gone on the picnic, local people and the police searched all over the rocky ground. They found blood stains on a rock. Some people took courage and climbed further down to locate the smashed body and were shocked…

The Inspector said, "Move, move away. Is this man a member of your party?"

"Yes Sir."

"What's the name?"

"Vijaysarthy."

ALSO **READ**

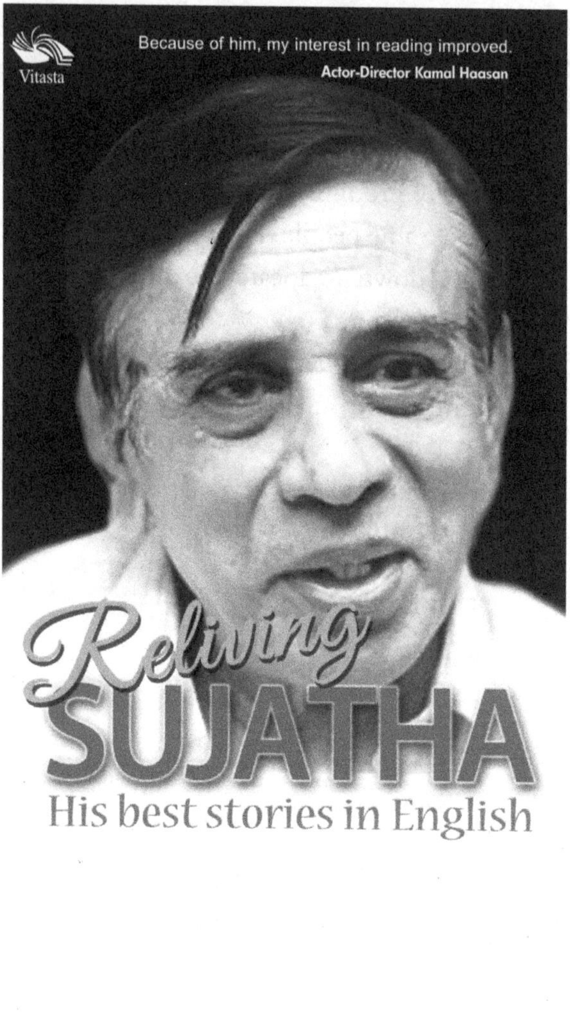

Vitasta
Because of him, my interest in reading improved.
Actor-Director Kamal Haasan
Reliving
SUJATHA
His best stories in English